All my Firsts:
Passion and Heartache

Nora O. Eigil

Dedicated to Simon, Damian and "Victor"

for giving me memories that will stay with me forever ♥

All my Firsts: Passion and Heartache

Nora O. Eigil

Published by Nora O. Eigil, 2023.

ALL MY FIRSTS: PASSION AND HEARTACHE

First edition. August 29, 2023.

Copyright © 2023 Nora O. Eigil.

ISBN: 979-8223328698

Written by Nora O. Eigil.

Chapter 1.

The first month in New York City had not been easy. I was never really a city girl, and the smell and noise of New York City were overwhelming to me. But the city slowly started to grow on me as I got more familiar with the streets near the hotel, where I lived and worked. I had landed a job as Junior VIP Manager at the impressive and luxurious Imperial Towers Hotel in Manhattan. I felt more than lucky to have this opportunity, especially without the educational background that most VIP managers at the large hotels had. I had never imagined I would end up in New York or working in the hotel business for this long.

My gap year was supposed to only be one year working as a hotel waitress in Surrey, England, before going to university in Copenhagen to study. But one gap year turned into three as I fell deeply in love with the hospitality world. I worked in England for a year and continued on to hotels in Bali, Ireland, and back to England, this time in London.

Early on in my gap year, I decided that I wouldn't return to Denmark to study at the university. Instead, my eyes were set on the prestigious École Hôtelière de Lausanne in Switzerland. But I needed money—a hell of a lot of money, actually—to pay the tuition fee. And that was where Matt's call changed everything. He argued that at a luxury hotel in Manhattan, I would make a much better salary, get much better tips, and get the right recommendations on my resume to get into the school. I booked the plane tickets as soon as we hung up. I was good at making quick decisions. Some would say I was too good. I was impulsive, rootless, quickly bored, and had a chronic feeling of loneliness that always had me looking for excitement to fill the void. Much too often, I would get myself into trouble by acting first and thinking later. But so far, this decision seemed like one of my best ones. Matt had been right on point. He usually was. That's why I liked him.

We had met at the hotel in London, where I worked as head waitress. Matt had been the hotel manager. It was a smaller hotel than the Imperial Towers and definitely not as extravagant, but still high-class with VIP guests. Matt was ambitious and smart, and he had an excellent talent for catering to high-profile guests and making them feel at home. We were both born with a talent for hospitality and impeccable service, and Matt had early on noticed my keen interest in creating a career in this field and had taken me under his wing. He had been an important mentor for me and had established a training program for me. I had grown quite attached to him, even if you wouldn't call us close friends. Unfortunately, he was offered an amazing job opportunity after a year and moved on to bigger and better things in New York. So, when he called me about the job, I threw what I had in my hands and packed my bags. The job as Junior VIP Manager was the perfect job for me. I had plenty of experience dealing with demanding guests who loved to complain and find flaws just to consolidate their power. I had an eye for details, and I knew what the guests wanted before they even knew it themselves. I had great recommendations from everyone I had ever worked with. It came naturally to me to work hard, and I just wanted to be the best at what I did and learn as much as I could, mostly because I had this big dream of running my own small resort or hotel one day.

"Hey Leonora, are you off now?" A voice behind me startled me.

It was Alwyn. He smiled. He always seemed to pop up out of nowhere and startle me. More so today. Alwyn was one of the guys who was obviously hoping for a chance with me. I was insecure and had never really liked the girl looking back at me in the mirror, but once out on my own in the big world, I quickly realized that I had a magnetic effect on the opposite sex. And I used it because it made me feel less lonely. Beautiful, funny, outgoing, clever, attentive, and mirthful. That was how I was described over and over again by everyone who met me. It sounds great, doesn't it? And behind all that was a girl with issues. Scared of intimacy, lacking self-esteem, and borderline self-destructive at times. Despite my flirting, he really wasn't my type. Well, I'm not sure I really had a type, but my walls were high and impossible for most guys to break through.

I smiled back. "No, I am just going down to my room to get some things."

"We are never off at the same time," Alwyn sighed.

I laughed and smiled at him. "Good things come to those who wait."

I winked and laughed.

I ran down the stairs to the staff quarters before he could say anything.

As luxurious and spacious everything was upstairs, just as cramped and dark everything was here in the basement of the hotel, where the staff quarters were. Small rooms with no windows. The rooms had just space for a bed, a dresser, and a shower and sink. That's it. But this was New York City; we couldn't really ask for better accommodation, and besides, we were here to work. I brushed my hair and looked in the mirror. I had long Scandinavian hair, blond and wavy. I was 6 feet tall, athletic, and slim. I had a body most girls envied, but I always felt like a tower next to everyone else. I grew up feeling awkward and unattractive. Until one day at high school, a new teacher came in, and when his eyes fell on me, he blurted out, "You are beautiful!" I was mortified. And confused. But it slowly made me look at myself differently. When the most popular guy at school, without saying a word, drunkenly went straight over to me and kissed me deeply at a party and only hesitantly left my side when his friends pulled him away to go home, I realized that others definitely saw something that I couldn't.

My pager buzzed and got me back to the present. I checked that my uniform was spotless. Because of my small waist but long legs, my uniform skirts were much, much shorter on me than anyone else. Matt had been upset about my short skirt at first. It was short, I would give him that, but it wasn't my fault that the designer clearly hadn't realized that you could have a small waist and long legs at the same time. I dapped some lipstick on, grabbed my notebook and pen, and then went back up. There were so many things to remember: names and preferences, important details for specific rooms, etc. I was still getting to know the hotel.

I headed over to the stairs to the VIP floors, which were the floors from 15 and up. These were my areas. My job was to ensure that everything was always perfect and flawless on these floors and, of course, to serve the guests. I almost always took the stairs up to at least the 6th floor. Unless Damian was around, of course. Damian was a butler assistant, 19 years old, and refreshingly irresponsible. In my first week, he showed me how he would stop the elevator halfway between the different floors, pry the doors open, and have stashes of sweets and soda stocked in the wall cracks. I loved him. He made me laugh endlessly. So, if Damian was around, I would most definitely take the elevator with him. He was not around, though, so I took the stairs to the 8th floor before getting into the elevator. I liked my staircase exercise, but I also had to look presentable.

The 15th floor was stylish, bright, and had an amazing view. I could get lost in this skyline view. On this floor, we had our library room, the lounge area with its breathtaking terrace, and the fine dining restaurant at the other end. Our skyline view was exceptional, our bartenders and chefs were renowned, and this was the place to come.

. . . .

I WENT INTO THE LIBRARY room to set things up for the meeting. I loved the library. The soft scent of aged leather and the faint aroma of freshly brewed coffee from the station were comforting and relaxing. Large area rugs with intricate patterns provided a sense of warmth to the otherwise bright and modern setting. In the corner of the room were cozy areas with comfy Papa Bear Chairs, and at the heart of the room stood a grand oak table with Eames chairs around it. Soft classical music played gently in the background, enhancing the serene atmosphere. Every wall was naturally lined with books of all genres. I was a bit of a bookworm and loved to go through the books and even take one or two back to my room to read. I set up the cigar table and filled the tray with cold water and a bottle of our finest whiskey. I checked to make sure no fingermarks were on any surfaces, that the glasses were immaculately clean, and that all the books were completely aligned. I placed some bowls with granola bites as well as dried fruits and nuts next to the whiskey. Finally, I rearranged the fresh flowers and looked around, pleased with the room. The library was most definitely ready for the board of directors.

As I was leaving the room, two tall young men walked in. From their features, it was apparent that they were brothers. They held a certain air of confidence, which, as I had come to recognize, comes with money and a privileged upbringing. Their dark, neatly styled hair and clean-shaven faces added to their polished appearance, which was played up by their tailored navy-blue suits. They smiled and nodded at me. I hadn't seen them before. I surely would have noticed them, as they were both striking men, probably only a little bit older than me. Four older, distinguished men followed soon after into the library. They radiated power and wealth. I gathered one of them would be Mr. Oppenheim, the founder of the Oppenheim Group, although I could not tell which one he was.

Guests were beginning to come into the lounge, and it was time for me to circulate among them while still being close to the library should the board of directors require special attention. Just as I was heading over to talk to Leon and Maria to get details about the guests that were already seated, the elevator opened, and a man walked with steady steps to the library. He turned around as if he could feel my stare. He had olive colored skin, short, dark brown hair, and a tight, white shirt that all too well revealed his muscular build. Our eyes met, and a sudden jolt of electricity coursed through me. I tried to look away, to divert my attention elsewhere, but it was as if an invisible force held my gaze captive. He seemed aware of the effect he had on me, and a confident smile played on his lips. His eyes traced my form, up and down, as if he could read my thoughts, stirring a blush on my cheeks. Despite my best efforts to appear composed, I couldn't help but feel flustered under his penetrating gaze. As he walked on and into the library, I realized I shouldn't have stared like that, and I tried to compose myself.

I looked for Maria and found her smiling at me from the bar. I liked Maria. She was 26, five years older than me, and an incredible bartender and sommelier. She was mixing up some beautiful cocktails when I came over.

"So, you met the Oppenheims," she said, nodding her head towards the library. "Good-looking family, right? I saw you staring at Victor," she laughed. "Don't worry, we all do! Arthur and Phillip are gorgeous, but Victor, he is so handsome... umm... and with that bad boy aura."

Maria licked her lips as a joke, and we giggled.

"So, Arthur and Phillip are the younger brothers? And Victor is the big brother?"

"Yes, Phillip had his 24th birthday party in the banquet room a few months ago. It took days to clean up after that party! But he seems like a good guy. I'm not sure how old Arthur is. I googled it once. I think he might be 21 like you. Victor is 32. I know that for a fact, because he had Leon and me create custom drinks for his birthday dinner in June. I have to make one of them for you once, they were really nice!"

I really wanted to ask questions about Victor, but I didn't want to show my interest. As if she could read my mind, she looked at me with a serious look.

"Victor is sexy, but he leaves a trail of broken women behind him, so stay clear. If you really must, go for Phillip. At least he is single," she teased.

I made a grimace to show her that I had all intentions of staying far away. As a matter of fact, there was no risk of me getting involved with anyone.

. . . .

IT WOULD BE A BUSY day at the lounge area today. The weather was beautiful, and it was perfect for dining and drinking on the big terrace. We pulled the glass doors to the side, so the lounge opened up completely to the terrace, removing boundaries between inside and out. I loved it. It was absolutely beautiful. I enjoyed the view for a few minutes and went over to Leon and Maria to look at the guest list today. There were so many names and details to remember, so I dotted them down in my notebook.

. . . .

THE BOARD MEETING WAS over, and the older men walked out deep in conversation. Matt made a sign for me to come over to him. "I want to introduce you to Victor Oppenheim, our CEO, and the head of the Oppenheim Group. He has been out of the office this past month. His brothers should be in there as well. They don't have an active role in the hotel, but Phillip will soon be taking on more responsibilities. Currently, Victor's main priority within the group lies in improving and expanding the hotel chain; when his work is done, Phillip will step in as president for the hotels. Phillip is still only here occasionally, so it will be best for you to get acquainted with them all right now."

I walked behind Matt, feeling a bit nervous.

The three men were still there, relaxing in the armchairs with whiskey in their glasses. The two younger brothers were vividly talking and smiled at us as we came in. "Matthew! Good to see you again!" One of them got up and hugged Matt.

"This is Phillip," Matt said. Phillip was a good-looking guy with friendly eyes and striking features. "This is Leonora, my VIP Junior Manager. She will take good care of all of you when I am not around," Matt said politely.

"Well, we might just have to be here more often then, right, Phillip?" Arthur grinned and looked over at Phillip.

I smiled at them and reached out for a handshake, but Arthur was quick to lift my hand up to his mouth and give it a gallant kiss with a cheeky smile. I felt uncomfortable by the gesture but smiled. At least Matt was here with me.

Someone else was in the room with us as well. His presence filled the room, demanding attention without saying a word.

"Welcome to the Imperial Towers Hotel then, Leonora. We have already met."

The flirtatious voice came from the corner. I looked at him, embarrassed by being called out for staring at him earlier. He was strikingly handsome and masculine, with a powerful physique and a magnetic presence. His masculine aura was enhanced by his dark hair, a confident smile, and an intensity in his eyes. He looked like trouble. He looked like everything in my wildest dreams and everything I knew to stay very far from. He had a playful spark in his eye, but nothing else revealed the nature of the teasing comment. I mumbled something I couldn't quite understand myself.

"Where are you from?" he said, looking curiously at me.

"I'm from Denmark." I wanted to say so much more. I wanted to be quick-witted, but I couldn't. His intense presence made me feel so insecure and bewildered.

He smiled at me. "Well, then welcome to New York City, Miss Denmark. I'm Victor, your CEO," he said, studying my face intensely.

I blushed. Matt, Arthur, and Phillip got back to talking about last night's game. I wanted to get out again.

"Matthew, I'm entertaining guests tonight. Please make sure that everything is perfect." Victor interrupted their chat. He then nodded to the door, which was our cue to leave.

When we came out, I breathed a sigh of relief. I was used to being around crazy rich people, famous people, eccentric people and most definitely rude people, but not someone with such a strong presence that had a physical impact on me.

"Take notes," Matt said, "Victor often stays in the penthouse. I will show you what he requests for his social gatherings, so you can set it up next time, and then you can go back. I will be off afterwards. Leon and Maria will be here for the rest of your shift."

· · · ·

HE TOOK ME TO A STORAGE room and filled a cart with bottles of Moët & Chandon and Dom Pérignon, two bottles of Balvenie whiskey, lots of glasses, and a box of cigars. Matt then made a call to the florist to have bouquets sent up, followed by an email to the kitchen for finger food. We took the staff elevator to the penthouse apartment. It was absolutely beautiful – modern and bright complimented with antique furniture. I loved it. The living area boasted floor-to-ceiling windows with a panoramic view of the most amazing skyline. Beige comfortably-looking oversized couches with throw pillows created an inviting and relaxing atmosphere in the living room. But the most breathtaking of it all, was the infinity pool that seemed to merge with the horizon on the private terrace. If I had free access to this suite, I would most definitely live here most of the time as well, I thought.

Matt began to set up the bar area and I went over to the open kitchen to touch the pristine white marble that reflected the natural light. Matt could tell I was overwhelmed with the beauty of the penthouse and chuckled "If you start saving now, you might spend a night here one day."

"I have never seen anything like it. I wish I had parents who would give me a hotel. Instead, all I got from them were issues to deal with the rest of my life," I answered sarcastically.

Matt and I had a strictly professional relationship and didn't share intimate details about our lives, but we had a strong connection, and of course, he knew I had my oddities. Most people only saw me as flirtatious, cheerful, and bubbly, but Matt had also seen my other side; sadness was always lurking under the surface, I couldn't always control my impulsivity, and that I liked, maybe too much at times, being on my own.

"Well, that's just what makes you so unique and fascinating. And let's not forget, they gave you brains as well. I have never met anyone as knowledgeable as you!" he said with a sweet, comforting smile.

Matt was really a great mentor and manager, always supportive and encouraging.

I laughed, "Speaking of! I'm reading Greek myths at the moment. Did you know that Medusa wasn't always a hideous monster? She was actually a very beautiful priestess of Athena."

"Tell me more," Matt laughed, "but please do so while you set up the terrace. Let's expect 20 guests."

I went out on the terrace, which was a masterpiece of design. The terrace itself was a seamless extension of the penthouse, with panoramic sliding doors. Lush greenery and meticulously maintained bushes lined the terrace. Sculpted topiaries, fragrant flowers, and cascading vines provided small cozy zones furnished with comfy couches and loungers.

I shouted to Matt in the living room while making notes on the list. "Okay, so Athena demanded all her priestesses to be virgins and dedicate their lives fully to her. Athena and Poseidon were enemies. Poseidon had heard about Medusa, Athena's beautiful priestess, and decided to seduce her to spite and humiliate Athena. Some say Medusa was raped, others say she was seduced.

"But nevertheless, it all happened right inside Athena's temple. The most sacrilegious act of all. Athena was furious, and she couldn't go after Poseidon, who was a powerful god, so she punished Medusa for disobedience. She cursed her for breaking her oath of celibacy by making sure no one would ever be able to look at her again.

"And we all know the story of her snake hair and eyes that would turn you to stone. Sad story, isn't it? I have been thinking about the lesson of the story and..."

I noticed Matt had gone all quiet. I went back into the living area to look for him. He wasn't there.

"Most people talk to themselves quietly. But not you. You shout out Greek stories to yourself. Very impressive."

I turned around. Victor sat in the armchair behind me. My heart skipped a beat, caught off guard by his unexpected appearance. He really was perfection. He radiated masculinity and confidence as he sat there casually in the armchair. His grey eyes had a playful spark to them, and the beautifully formed lips curved into a hint of a mischievous smile. My cheeks turned crimson with embarrassment. I was unable to say anything. He grinned at my flustered reaction.

"Oh no, no, I was talking to Matt. He was right here."

"Hmm, sure. Let's call it that then, 'Talking to Matt'. But just to be sure, is Matt standing here with us right now?" he asked teasingly.

I gave in to the joke and giggled.

He continued. "Well, don't leave me with such a cliffhanger to the story. I sat here, all excited for the big finish. Will you share the moral of the story?"

I was hoping he was still joking, but by the look of it, he wasn't. I took a few breaths and gathered myself.

"I think the intended lesson is that once we do something bad, it changes our character," I replied.

"Interesting." He seemed to reflect on it and nodded his head in agreement. "A very classic interpretation. If we look at it from a modern business perspective, I think the lesson is: never go against your superior," he said while emphasizing never and drew two fingers across his throat. I laughed at his joke, surprised that he actually was funny. I could feel myself relaxing a bit more now, although I was still very tense.

"Okay, if we are looking at it from that perspective, it could also be that if you associate with rival companies, it will get you in serious trouble," I said.

"Yes! I definitely agree with that one," he chuckled. Then he grinned playfully. "It's better than 'don't ever have sex at the office' which I was going to suggest." He winked.

"Well, that's a good policy, even today. Let's go for that one," I said, looking around, hoping Matt would show up soon.

He laughed at my obvious uneasiness.

"You're looking for Matthew?" He got up.

He was tall, probably 6 ft 2, broad-shouldered, and his shirt was unable to hide the contours of his muscles.

"Would you like a drink while we wait for him? I would love to hear more stories."

"Oh no, I can't. I better finish my list. I just came to check on Matt."

Right then, Matt walked in, and I felt so relieved and thankful. Matt had a cart packed with vases with beautiful flowers. The enchanting scent of lilies and roses quickly filled the room.

"Victor," Matt said surprised. "I'm sorry, I didn't expect you already. We will hurry up," he said while making a nodding gesture, which I interpreted as 'get moving!'

"Don't mind me. Leonora is giving me old Greek advice on how to run a business. It's much appreciated."

Matt looked at me confused, but I was just so relieved to get away, that I made a dismissive wave and went to check the other rooms, while Matt continued talking to Victor. 20 minutes later, we were done, and I had completed the list for housekeeping and the kitchen. Victor was occupied with a business call out on the terrace, so we left quietly without a word.

. . . .

LEON WAS MIXING DRINKS when I came back, and Simon and Damian had cleared the library. Maria was busy serving the guests. She smiled when she came back. "Brace yourself," she said while looking smugly at Leon. "The three evil stepsisters are here."

Leon winked at me, "Don't worry, they love me, don't listen to Maria."

Maria pointed discreetly to a table with three elderly ladies and she gestured for me to come closer as she whispered, "In all seriousness, they are evil. They complain about everything, and I can assure you that you will be busy with them all afternoon. They have come here regularly for years, probably decades, for our afternoon tea. Old money, you know. Leon can introduce you, because he can literally do no wrong in their eyes." I looked over at Leon, who had a big, smug smile on his face.

"What can I say?" he grinned. I understood why they liked Leon. He was charming and funny, and his South-African accent had a pleasing effect on us all. He was in his late 20's, and his incredible waiting and bartending skills could probably impress even the most disagreeable old ladies.

Leon led me to their table and introduced me. They weren't quite as bad as Maria had painted them. I stayed with them for over half an hour chatting about how the hotel had changed over the years. Small talk came naturally to me and I dove into conversations with a genuine interest in the other person, which gave me the ability to charm almost anyone - when I chose to. The ladies were so enthusiastic about our conversation that they announced they would bring photographs to show me at their next visit. Maria rolled her eyes discreetly at me, when I walked past her with a triumphant leer.

It was a particularly busy afternoon and evening with VIP and Elite guests, and I was so deeply exhausted from trying to remember names, positions, relations etc. All I wanted to do was just sleep. Finally, the clock hit 9 pm, and I waved goodbye to Maria and Leon and went for a final round to make sure everything was perfect.

At the opposite end of the lounge area, restaurant and library, we had the corridor down to the fitness room. Everything was fine, and I went upstairs. The 16th floor had the management offices as well as a break- and meeting room for those of us who worked on the VIP floors. Matt and I also shared a small office here. Further down, we had our two spacious and elegant banquet rooms. The 16th floor was wonderfully quiet at this time of the hour. I went down to the end of the floor. Here guests could recline on large oversized couches, surrounded by luxurious plant arrangements, while admiring the breathtaking views from the vast panoramic windows. Gentle nature sounds played softly from the speakers. I let myself slide to the floor and just take in the breathtaking view of New York. I could hear the elevator doors open and someone walk determinedly to where I was.

"Hey, I knew you were here. I have to go unpack some suitcases. Please join me?"

It was Damian. I was so tired, but Damian could always make me smile, so I nodded and got up.

We went over to the elevator, and he looked at me, "Thirsty or hungry?"

I laughed out loud. "Hmm, thirsty, I think. Coke zero, please."

"Of course, 18th floor, it is then." Halfway between the 17th and 18th floor, he put his fingers behind the door and pushed it open. The elevator stopped and revealed a brick wall with rock shelves with neatly placed cans of soda. He took one out, opened it, and handed it to me.

I giggled. "You are going to get fired one day."

"I know, but until then I won't be hungry or thirsty, right?"

Despite his obvious laidback and untroubled approach to life, he really was on the way to becoming a great butler. Liked by all, loved by me.

We went back down to the 17th floor into a Junior Suite. The bell boy had brought two full luggage carts to the room. Damian took a beautiful brown leather suitcase down and put it on the luggage stand and opened it.

"I will never understand why anyone would want a complete stranger to go through their personal stuff," I said.

"If they knew I always sniff their underpants, I am sure they wouldn't ask for it," he said while looking all serious at me.

I giggled. I laid on the floor, while Damian jokily sniffed underpants, tried on jackets and bras. I was amused and worried at the same time that someone should walk in on us.

"Damian, you are freaking me out now. I am about to have a panic attack. Stop it. Finish up and let's go."

He did an eyeroll at me and smiled. "You know what you need? A boyfriend. Someone like me," he said.

I chortled. "Damian!"

Everything was just fun and uncomplicated with Damian and Simon, which is why I sought out their company all the time, despite they were a bit younger than me. They always made me laugh. Damian was cheeky and just as flirtatious as me. Full on. He had a girlfriend, but always claimed he was more than willing to dump her, if I just said the word. It was a game between us. It made me laugh so much, which at times upset him, nevertheless, we continued the game almost every day. He wasn't creepy like so many guys.

"Well, maybe one day. Right now, I just want to get out of here. Let's go find Simon and have dinner."

We took the elevator down to the basement to the staff dining area. Staff breakfast was always baked beans and toast. Lunch was the same. Dinner was usually better as it was leftovers from guest lunch. I filled my plate with some potatoes and legumes and went over to the table with the girls from housekeeping. Damian and Simon followed and quickly began chatting up the girls. I was going over the day in my head. The magnetic field around Victor had been so strong. And I ended up embarrassing myself with my Medusa-story.

"Did you hear me," Alwyn said.

"Pardon?" I must have drifted away in my thoughts. He reiterated his monologue about the big wedding party at the end of the week. I really was too tired to listen, so I just nodded and tried to smile or look sympathetic once in a while. I quickly finished my dinner, wished them all a goodnight, and went back to my room to sleep.

. . . .

MY ALARM CLOCK WOKE me up at 5 a.m. I sneaked out of my room and up to the 15th floor. Everything was still quiet. I used my key card to open the door to the fitness room. I had been sneaking into the fitness room since my first day. I did my Pilates routine and then half an hour on the cross machine every day – this hour sometimes felt like the best time of my day with my body and mind completely in sync. It was nearly 6 a.m. now, so I finished off before any guests might come down to do an early training session. Back in my room, I took a long shower, braided my hair, put orange nail paint on my toes, slipped on my stockings and underwear, and then put on my uniform and black shoes.

Leon, Simon and Damian came out from their rooms almost at the same time as I did, and we joked and chatted on the way to the dining area to get our baked beans. I enjoyed these mornings when we had breakfast together. That was one of the things I loved about this 24-hour work life. We talked about the Australian couple who stayed in one of the suites, and soon Simon and Damian were in a heated discussion about whether Sydney or Melbourne was the capital of Australia.

I rolled my eyes at them. "You are embarrassing to listen to! It's Canberra!"
Leon laughed, "I think she is right."

I shook my head in exaggerated disbelief, left the table to put the dirty plates away, and went back to my room to brush my teeth. It felt like the beginning of a good day. I would be off already at 3 p.m. today, which meant I could go out sightseeing a bit.

The day passed quickly. I spent most of the morning in the shared office with Matt, going through this month's Elite and VIP issues and writing reports. In the afternoon, I went around to check if the issues had been resolved up to standard. At 3 p.m., not a minute later, I closed the door to the office and hurried down the stairs. I wanted to get out of here as quickly as possible, so I skipped my shower and just quickly changed into jeans and a top. I took the staff exit through the underground parking garage and ran up the stairs to the streets.

The sharp honks of taxis and the blaring sirens of emergency vehicles were overwhelming. The tranquility inside the Imperial Towers was in stark contrast to the noise outside. Some people loved the cacophony of sounds in the city, but to me, it was noise. Swiftly, I made my way to the nearest avenue in search of the bus stop for Bx29 to take me to City Island. After reading about it on a travel website, City Island instantly made it to my list of places I had to visit. I didn't have to wait long before the bus arrived. Bx29 took me through various neighborhoods in the Bronx to the scenic tree-lined drive into City Island.

Charming storefronts, art galleries, clapboard houses adorned with vibrant flowers, Victorian-style cottages lining the waterfront, and the scent of saltwater welcomed me as I stepped out of the bus. It was absolutely beautiful, tranquil and as if time stood still here in this hidden New York gem. I walked down to the harbor to look at the sailboats and fishing vessels. The rhythmic creaking of boat masts and the gentle lapping of waves against the docks created a soothing sound. I sat here for a while, completely lost in thoughts, while the sun warmed my body. Finally, I got up and walked down to the sandy beach. Families were building sandcastles, and couples taking romantic strolls along the water's edge. I buried my feet in the warm sand and lay down while seagulls glided gracefully above me. The sunset cast a warm and golden glow over the beach, creating a breathtaking finale to my day. It was time to head back.

. . . .

I WOKE UP FEELING REFRESHED, even before the alarm clock rang. After my workout and breakfast, I went back to my room to put on some music and tidy up a bit. Although the staff accommodation was devoid of windows, I had managed to give my room a homely feeling. The walls were plain white, except for one wall, where I had put wallpaper on with a lively botanical pattern showcasing lush exotic plants, brightly colored blossoms, and palm trees. The colors spanned from shades of green and turquoise to vibrant yellow and red. It made me happy each time I looked at it. In one corner of the room, next to the door, was a compact shower area. Adjacent to the shower was a sink atop a countertop with a mirror above it. Of course, the main piece of furniture in the small room was my bed, positioned against one wall. Next to the bed and across from the sink was a set of drawers for my clothes and personal belongings. Usually, management, even junior management, was expected to provide their own accommodation, but as I was an undocumented immigrant, Matt had pulled some strings. A knock on my door interrupted my cleaning, and I opened the door to see Maria smiling outside.

"I could hear your music. Are you ready for work?"

I nodded and closed the door behind me.

As we made our way to the staff meeting, I filled her in on every detail of City Island and how amazing it had been. We were the first to arrive, so we sat down and waited for the others to show up. Damian and Simon strolled in, joking with some of the other butlers, and quickly the rest followed, first some of the waiters, then the restaurant manager and the sous chef, and finally Matt. Our staff meetings were usually smaller, but we had a big wedding coming up this week. The chef and the restaurant manager presented the menu and discussed the details regarding the wedding dinner, and Matt talked through the guests and their room requests with the butlers. My job was to keep the bride and groom happy and be close by at all times to the wedding planner to make sure all requests and issues were dealt with quickly. Maria and I were excited about taking part in a socialite wedding, even if we were just outside spectators, and decided we would help each other style our hair for the event. Except for the wedding, it would be a slow week, which suited me well, as Matt had assigned me the responsibility of conducting a competitor analysis. Once the meeting had finished, Maria and I went down to the lounge. Leon was already busy stocking up the bar, while chatting to one of our regular guests. Maria went over to help Leon out, and I went out on the terrace to make sure everything was picture-perfect.

I walked back in and quickly scanned the lounge. Something caught my eye on the floor by one of the sofas, and I went over to pick it up. Wasabi peas. I was hungry, and I loved wasabi peas. Some people lived by the 'One Second Rule'. Not me, never had. 'The 3 Months Rule', perhaps. I picked them up and put them in my mouth, savoring the burning sensation. Someone coughed politely behind me. I turned around and looked straight into two strikingly playful gray eyes. Victor. Mesmerizingly sexy and handsome Victor. He didn't take his eyes off me. I debated with myself whether or not to spit the peas out or swallow them. I swallowed, hoping their disappearance would make him and the uncomfortable situation go away.

"That's one way to clean the room," he said with his gaze fixed on me with intensity.

"Yes, I am very dedicated to my job," I replied. "No need for a vacuum cleaner, when you have me. And another bonus, if you ever happen to strand on a desert island, just take me with you, and I am sure to find us something to eat," I said, hoping this conversation would soon be over. He made me nervous, and when I was nervous, my mouth would just babble. His beautifully formed lips let out a laugh. Right then, I realized how even more awkward it would have been, if he had no sense of humor. I was relieved.

"Can I get you anything?" I said and put on my professional face and polite smile.

He sat down in a dark olive colored Papa Bear chair. "I am meeting someone here in a few minutes. A glass of whiskey, please, for me and a glass of champagne for my date," he said. Adding a subtle smile and a wink, he playfully remarked, "Oh, and some wasabi peas. Not from the floor, though, please, if you don't mind."

I smiled politely, pretending not to be embarrassed, and went over to the bar to pass on the request to Leon.

I went to get my laptop in the office and went back to the lounge to find a quiet place in the corner to work on my competitor analysis. It helped me to be right here, surrounded by the very segment, I was researching. Once in a while, my attention was drawn to Victor on the opposite end of the lounge area. His date had arrived. She was impeccable. Her hair was impeccable, her blue pencil dress was impeccable, her makeup was impeccable, and her overall appearance was impeccable. Only wealth could bring about this level of perfection. They made an odd, but perfect couple. His raw masculinity and commanding aura and her flawless look were conflicting, yet it was obvious that they made a strong couple among the New York elite.

I redirected my attention to my research once again. Hours passed without me even noticing the world around me, and eventually Maria came over and suggested I go down to get some late lunch. No one else was in the dining area, so I finished quickly and went to my room for a few minutes. I looked in the mirror. I wished I could look as impeccable, as the woman did. My wavy locks constantly attempted to escape my carefully made braid, freckles adorned my nose like a sprinkle of stardust, and while I wished I were the type to wear classic red nail paint, I always ended up applying bold and vivid colors to my nails. I was certainly not impeccable.

I went back up to the lounge. Just a handful of guests were seated in the restaurant, and in the lounge, five men in dark suits were discussing their businesses vividly. The lounge was peaceful before the post-dinner drink rush. I went behind the bar looking for some notes, Matt should have left me, when

Simon and Damian sneaked up on me. I was in a teasing mood, so I slowly leaned towards Damian with a suggestive smile and put my hand on his arm. "I forgot to tell you. I had a wet dream about you last night," I purred.

"Yeah?" he said eagerly. "Umm, you got hit by a bus...and I wet myself laughing!" I burst out. Damian's disappointed face was priceless, and Simon and I couldn't stop laughing.

"For a second, I thought you were serious! You just broke my heart!" he exclaimed in a dramatic manner.

I heard a suppressed laugh, and turned my attention in its direction. At the end of the bar, Victor sat, observing us intently, his lips betraying a subtle smile. None of us had seen him sitting there, and we quickly stood up straight, knowing this was not the time or place to be joking around like that.

"I am sure you all have tasks awaiting your attention elsewhere right now," he said with a serious expression.

"I am sorry," I murmured, feeling a touch of embarrassment from being caught. I wasn't exactly presenting myself in the most flattering light to the CEO these days.

"No worries, Leonora," he reassured, before he playfully added, "but didn't we just talk yesterday about the devastating consequences of being inappropriate at work?"

Simon and Damian swiftly dispersed, just as I realized Victor wasn't actually mad. I smiled in relief as our eyes locked.

• • • •

THE NIGHT OF THE WEDDING party had finally arrived, and Maria and I were excited about experiencing a bit of romance. We had fun getting ready in my room. With the help of YouTube, Maria did my hair with two side braids and a low bun, and I gave her a sleek straight hair updo. Pleased with the results of our newly acquired hairdressing skills, we moved on to the makeup that we kept subtle, but romantic. Matt had kindly given us a 30-minute break to get into the wedding feel, which wasn't much time, but we made it back to the 16th floor just before our break was over. I found the wedding planner, who I had already talked to several times the past few days. We went through a few details, she wasn't pleased about, and I hoped the rest of the evening would pass without issues.

Thankfully, everything went smoothly and I was pleasantly surprised to find that my presence was needless for the rest of the night, and so I spent most of the time either chatting with guests or enjoying the stillness in the dark and quiet corners of the hotel where I could enjoy the strange New York City night sky. As I was resting my head against the windows, looking at the night sky, a man and a woman appeared from the shadows further down the corridor. They hadn't seen me. Her beautiful pink dress revealed she was a wedding guest. She had both her hands on the man's chest and her intentions were very much evident. He leaned in towards her and said something that made her giggle. I couldn't help looking at them and their flirtatious behavior. They slowly made their way towards the area where I stood. I wanted to hide, but there really wasn't anywhere to hide. I prepared to excuse myself hoping they would be quickly on their way. I mean, it was obvious what they were up to this far from the wedding party, they should be wanting to get out of this awkward situation just as much.

As they came closer, I realized the man was Victor. That same instant, he saw me too. Confused, I looked at the woman. She was pretty with a heavily made-up face and big boobs that had to be almost impossible to find clothes to fit in to. A strange feeling of slight envy crept over me, and I pictured what it would be like to feel his body pressed against mine.

"Hi, I was just about to leave," I stuttered while showing my best professional smile.

Victor let his hands on the woman go, but she was not ready to give up on her fresh catch and pulled herself closer towards him, while we all stood there staring at each other. He didn't seem to pay any attention to her anymore, but kept his eyes on me. He didn't say anything.

"I better finish my round," I said, and moved past them. I could hear the woman giggle and whisper something to Victor again, but he was quiet.

Suddenly, I heard him call out. "Wait, I'll go with you. I have some work to finish off as well."

Feeling very awkward, I walked off with Victor, leaving the woman behind.

• • • •

THE NEXT TWO WEEKS went by quickly. I was busy with the competitor analysis as well as trying hard to be present and engaged with our VIP guests, which we had had a lot of over the past two weeks. Today was quieter, and Maria and I were both off at 3 p.m. and excited to go visit the catacombs. Victor entered the lounge, taking a seat in the corner in a Wegner armchair with his laptop and mobile phone. He greeted us with a smile as he went past.

"I swear, he comes here just because of you." Maria nodded toward him. "We usually don't see much of him outside his office, but now he is here all the time. Did you know that he is asking questions about you? I think you have caught his attention."

I blushed. I couldn't deny the strong attraction, I had to him. Whenever he entered the room, his presence seemed to spark electric pulses in my skin.

She gave me a warning look. "Just be careful. Nothing good will come out of being his next prey."

I tried to ignore his presence the rest of the afternoon and not look in his direction, but I could feel his gaze on me. I was actually relieved when he went into the library with a man in a dark grey suit and asked Maria to close it off for his meeting. Maybe half an hour later, the impeccable woman from the previous day entered the lounge with some girlfriends. "Elizabeth is here," Maria nodded in the woman's direction. "Victor's fiancé. I don't think I ever see her smile. I know I would have a big smile on my face every day, if I slept with Victor!" Maria quipped.

"Shh!" I scolded Maria.

"Well, you can go over to them and get their orders, and I am sure you will come back and agree with me," she said.

I went over to the group, presented myself, and asked to take their orders. Elizabeth was the queen of perfection, but her girlfriends definitely had the same aura and look of impeccability. They were an intimidating group for sure, and I felt confident that it was almost impossible to be accepted by them, if you didn't have money and position. They barely acknowledged me. I went back to Maria with their orders. She mixed their drinks with care – and a grin - and arranged them beautifully on a tray, and handed it to me.

"Go make some friends now, Leonora," she said jestingly.

I served their drinks with a big smile, and not one of them looked up or thanked me.

ALL MY FIRSTS: PASSION AND HEARTACHE

"I told you!" Maria laughed, when I came back with the tray.

Chapter 2.

Although I looked for Victor, I didn't see him for a week. He was most likely busy with the upcoming grand opening of the new sister hotel, Parkview Palace. A charity event at the opening was the talk of the town among the socialites. We were busy too at Imperial Towers. The prince of Swaziland had announced his arrival later today, and he was bringing his entourage of 45 people. Matt was stressed. He had to call in extra butlers, have staff prepare the spa, and get masseurs and beauticians on standby. The prince came once or twice a year, so Matt already had a folder with his preferences and requirements, which eased his work, but the next couple of hours were nevertheless hectic. I was assigned the task of designating suites and rooms to the entourage based on their various relations and statuses. It was a complicated puzzle, but I managed to complete it to my own satisfaction.

Matt ran in and out of our office in a febrile state. Just 30 minutes before the estimated time of arrival, he came in and let himself fall back on his chair with a great sigh.

"We made it. What usually takes us a couple of days, we have achieved in 5 hours. I need a strong drink now! Can I get you one too?" he asked.

I smiled at him. He definitely deserved a drink.

"No, thank you, but I can go get one for you," I said and went downstairs to have Leon mix a surprise drink for Matt.

I came up with a pink and turquoise drink that Leon called the Stress Killer.

Matt looked rattled up again. "Victor just called. He needs me at the Parkview Palace urgently. I told him I can't because of the prince, so he is coming to pick you up in half an hour. I'm sorry, but it sounds like a late night for you too. Go get something to eat and wait for Victor in the parking garage. Don't let him wait."

I hurried down to the dining room and had some toast. I couldn't find anything else to eat right now, except the cold baked beans from today's lunch. 25 minutes later, I was ready for pickup. A sleek, black Audi swiftly raced down the ramp and came to an immediate stop before me. Victor got out, gave me a polite smile, and opened the door to the passenger seat. I tried to make myself comfortable in the seat, while I wondered if his mesmerizing effect on me was just as strong on anyone else.

He interrupted my thoughts. "I'm glad you could help. We have an issue at the Palace. I was not happy with the VIP manager and his team, so I let them go this morning. I have someone new to come in tomorrow, but we are on a tight schedule and can't miss a day. The hotel manager has taken most of the tasks upon himself, but I need you to go through the list of guests that are staying for the gala and check if their preference sheets match up with what has been set up in their rooms. I have cleared my schedule for today and will help you out."

He was clearly tense, but it only accentuated the dark erotism, he exuded. The rest of the drive was in silence. Victor seemed occupied in his own thoughts, and I simply didn't know what to say to him now that I found myself alone in a car with him.

We drove into the underground parking garage of the Parkview Palace, and he hurried out of the car to open the door for me. We went through the grand doors leading into the hall of the hotel. Stepping into the magnificent hall was like entering a parallel universe only for the rich. Large, strategically placed windows adorned the walls, inviting the sunlight to flood the interior and illuminate every corner. The ample use of glass created a seamless connection between the lavish interior and the busy world beyond. The floor was polished marble, reflecting the light and accentuating the bright ambiance. The furniture was a blend of modern and plush, designed for both comfort and style. Elegant sofas and armchairs in neutral tones harmonized with the soft color palette of the walls. I was completely taken away by the grandeur and beauty.

Victor placed his warm hand gently on my lower back, guiding me past the reception and lounge area, leading me towards the elevators. I was impressed by the elegance and luxury of the Imperial Towers, but this hotel was even more magnificent.

"I sense you like it," he said smiling as we went into the elevator.

I nodded. Pressing the button for the 4th floor, he leaned against the wall, his gaze fixed on me. I looked down, pretending not to notice his gaze.

We reached the floor, and he gestured for me to walk out first. Large windows along one side of the corridor allowed light to stream in to the opposite side that had large white doors leading in to the rooms. Seating areas were spaced out along the windowed side.

"Let's go through the rooms on this floor together, and then we can split the lists as we move on to the upper floors," he said.

While we checked the rooms in accordance with the preference sheets, Victor asked me about the progress of my analysis. I shared my findings and discussed some ideas with him, which was very rewarding. He was clearly a business wizard, and his suggestions were profoundly helpful to me. I was disappointed when we reached the final room on this floor and had to finish our conversation on the topic.

"You have some really great observations and ideas. I'm very impressed. Please come by my office any time, if you need any thoughts on the project," he said while he led me back to the elevator and up to the next floor.

Here he divided the lists between us and took the elevator further up.

On the 7th floor, he found me while I was writing small notes for the florists.

"There is a mix up in some of the junior suites. Can I see your list?"

He positioned himself close to me. Too close. Intimately close. The gentle touch of his jacket brushed against my arm, and his intoxicating scent enwrapped me. Neither of us made a move to step away. His hand brushed gently against mine, and I could feel electricity bolt through my body. Could he feel it too? I wasn't sure this very intimate closeness was an accident, as his hand touched mine for a few seconds too long.

None of us spoke, but eventually he broke the silence as he moved his hand and gently said, "It looks like four of the names on the preference sheets don't match with the rooms. We have to recreate the list."

I pulled myself together and focused on the lists, although it was difficult with him so close. Still, neither of us made a move to step away.

I studied the list leaning in towards him. "The couple in room 436 are in their 70s. I'm guessing they are the ones requesting twin beds with extra pillows. Wouldn't you say?" I suggested, trying to ignore how I could feel his warmth.

He broke our proximity in sudden glee. "I think you are right, and she wants light purple hydrangeas in the living room. That definitely sounds like an older woman," he beamed at me. "I'm putting Mr. and Mrs. Löwen down for room 436 then. Well done, you solved the first puzzle. Let's do the next one!"

The next three were harder. We tried to look each guest up on Facebook and Instagram to find some cues, but nothing revealed anything.

"We are wasting time. I'll ask reception to call them and have them confirm their preference sheets within tomorrow."

"Wait!" I exclaimed. "I got it. Lynda is a fashion influencer. She must be the one requesting a bright room with no direct sunlight, because she needs good light for her pictures. The others didn't look particularly active on social media. Also, the same couple has requested strawberries, cherries, and champagne to the room, which could be an Instagram prop?"

"You are good at this! Impressive. I'll trust you to figure out the last two. I have some business calls I need to make. I'll meet you down at the end," he replied before he began his call and left the room.

I didn't see him again before I had finished the final two floors. I was exhausted and relieved that I was heading back to bed soon.

"Sorry, I have some business in Dubai that required my attention. Come, let me show you the penthouse suite. I have ordered some late dinner for us."

Again, he put his hand on my lower back and led me to the elevator. The gesture felt both possessive and attentive at the same time, and I liked it. Entering the luxurious penthouse was nothing compared to feeling Victor's hand on my lower back and having him this close to me. It felt so wrong to be alone in the penthouse with him, but it was also so very tempting and arousing.

"Let's go out on the terrace," he said.

Out on the terrace, large lanterns with candlelight gave off a warm, flickering glow. Atop a tall concrete bar table, food had been meticulously arranged.

"I ordered vegan for you."

I looked at him in surprise. How did he know? A teasing, flirtatious smile curled on his lips. I decided it was better not to ask, so I let it go. I took a slice of bread and a small salad and sat down on the couch. I could feel the warm breeze on my skin. He took off his jacket and tie, and proceeded to loosen his shirt by undoing the upper buttons, before he sat down next to me.

"Thank you for your help today. You were brilliant," he smiled.

We made some light conversation about Parkview Palace and his disappointment in the VIP team. I tried to concentrate on the conversation, but the electricity in the air made it impossible. I felt dizzy, knowing that I had crossed a line when I entered the penthouse with him and that I might regret what would happen. His perfume was musky and sensual. His lips perfect.

Suddenly, but softly, he stroked the back of my neck. Then, he leaned slowly towards me; his eyes fixed on my lips. I sensed the impending moment, and a surge of anticipation washed over me. As he drew nearer, his warm breath grazed my skin, sending shivers down my spine. And then, he kissed me. He kissed my lips so softly and tenderly, before gently letting his warm tongue slide through my lips and play with my tongue. I had never been kissed like this before. I was more used to young guys' wet and hurried kisses than these slow, gentle kisses from an experienced man. I instinctively closed my eyes, surrendering myself to the sensations coursing through my veins. His intoxicating scent enveloped me, heightening my arousal even further. The deliberate exploration of his lips and tongue filled me with an insatiable longing for more. I couldn't help but release a soft giggle, overwhelmed by it all. He smiled back at me, and quietly resumed his tender kisses, drawing me back into his mesmerizing spell.

Suddenly, his phone rang. He ignored it at first, but eventually gave in to the persistent noise. It was as if the spell broke at that moment, and I panicked and got up. He tried to reach for my hand and pull me back, but whoever was on the other end of the phone was important enough for him to let me go. I don't remember how I got back down to the hall, but I ran out and into the streets of New York. I wasn't quite sure of the way back to the hotel, but I disappeared into the crowd, hoping I would be home soon.

• • • •

I WAS TERRIBLY TIRED the next morning. I had found my way home quicker than I thought I would, but I had barely slept. Confusion, excitement, and anxiety had kept me awake. I skipped both my workout and breakfast this morning, I just wanted to stay in bed today. I thought about calling in sick, but I also knew Matt would need me today. Reluctantly, I got up, showered, and got dressed. I could still feel Victor's warm kisses on my lips. I closed my eyes, thinking of him. How could something so wrong feel so good. It was obvious he was a ruthless heartbreaker, but the way he had kissed me so tenderly had made me feel special in a way, I had never felt. A sting in my heart revealed that no boyfriend had ever been so tender with me. I had to get Victor out of my mind. He was trouble. I could see the end to this even before it had begun. Most likely,

Victor would not be at the Imperial today, but I took no risks. Determined to avoid running into Victor on my own, I asked Matt if I could shadow him today with the prince, which Matt thought was a brilliant idea. So did I.

At just 9 in the morning, Victor made a sudden entrance into our office.

"Good morning," he smiled at both of us, but his gaze was on me.

His mischievous eyes were studying me intensely. A wave of relief washed over me as Matt quickly began to talk about the prince with Victor. He couldn't have done a better job blocking Victor, even if I had asked him. I blushed under Victor's continuous gaze, as vivid flashbacks flooded my mind: his kisses, his warmth, his alluring scent, and the intense, electrifying effect, he had on me. Matt and Victor went over to Matt's laptop to see something.

"Leonora, you should see this too," Matt said enthusiastically.

Victor took a step back to make room for me, and I reluctantly walked over to Matt's desk. Victor was so close to me. I could feel him behind me. I so desperately wanted to lean back against his chest or have him stroke me. To feel his naked, muscular chest and feel the strength of his arms around my waist in a promise of both protection and passion.

"Leonora!"

I had not heard Matt talk at all. Out of the corner of my eye, I could see a smile playing on Victor's lips. He knew exactly why I was distracted, and he enjoyed it.

"I'm sorry. I...I'm tired. Could you please repeat?"

I could sink into a hole right now. They were both looking at me now, one with a cheeky smile and the other slightly irritated. Matt repeated his question, and I concentrated fully on his face to answer without distraction. I went back to my chair and tried to hide behind my computer screens.

Eventually, Victor left, probably disappointed in how seemingly immature and inexperienced I came off. Although, I knew he had gone back to Parkview Palace, I shadowed Matt throughout the day, like a little scared puppy with separation anxiety. I fell quickly asleep that night, but intense dreams kept waking me up.

• • • •

AS THE FOLLOWING DAY came to an end and Victor had not appeared, I couldn't help but feel disappointed in myself. Of course, a man like him would not waste more thoughts on a young girl like me, who seemed to run off scared by the first kiss. So, this was it. Feeling stupid and miserable, I went to my secret hideout at the end of the 16th floor once my shift was over. The sun was going down now, and the skyline had colors of black, blue, and pink. Slowly, everything was turning dark. The New York City lights took over as the sun disappeared. The lights had gone out in the corridor, turning my hideout into a truly magical spot. I sat there for a really long time without moving, just taking in the beautiful view. It's strange how the largest city in the world could make you feel so lonely. Suddenly, the lights were activated, and the corridor became well-lit. I assumed it was just Damian looking for me, so I turned my head and saw Victor walk into his office. I could hear him on his phone. On impulse, I got up and walked down to his office without hesitation.

His door was open, so I went inside and closed the door behind me. I had no game plan or idea what I would say to him. I simply reacted on instinct. He looked surprised when he saw me and quickly finished his call. Then he moved toward me, but stopped.

"Come closer," he said with a low and husky voice.

I felt hypnotized. Everything around me seemed a blur. I knew I should leave, but I didn't want to. As if my body was pulled by an invisible string, I moved slowly towards him.

As I came close, he lifted my chin gently with his thumb and kissed me softly. Everything swirled around me. His soft kisses quickly turned deeper and more passionate. I kissed him back with the same passion and intensity. My hands instinctively found their place on his chest, tracing the contours of his muscles, feeling the hardened peaks of his nipples. It was a body unlike any I had touched before, arousing a hunger within me that I couldn't contain. I sighed. I let my fingers move over his well-built shoulders and up to the nape of his neck. He pulled me even closer and held me so tight I could barely breathe, while kissing me deeply. His embrace was firm and possessive. Maybe we kissed for seconds, maybe for hours; time and place disappeared in this moment. I wanted to feel him so badly. Every fiber of my being cried out for him. Maybe he could sense my body tremble for him, because with one hand he quickly pulled my hair back, his teeth grazing my neck in a teasing bite, while his other hand moved my panties aside. An involuntary moan escaped my lips as his fingers slipped inside me, claiming me and sending me into a state of intense pleasure. I let out a small whimper. My body yearned for him to take possession of my body fully, while my thoughts struggled to retain control. I wanted him to continue, to take me completely, yet a whisper of caution held me back. I didn't want him to ever stop, but I knew I couldn't do this.

"Wait," I managed to whisper, gasping for breath.

He didn't wait. He didn't stop. He pressed himself against me. Dizzy, I looked into his eyes, which were foggy with desire.

"You are torturing me," he whispered, barely audible in my ear.

I tried to push his hand away, but I couldn't. He was too strong, and my body was not willing to put up the fight. I was torn between the desires that consumed me and a voice of reason. My body was betraying me, craving the ecstasy his lips and fingers promised, while my mind wrestled with the consequences.

"No, stop. Stop!" I could hear the words come out of my mouth, but I don't know how I ever gathered the strength.

He let out a deep exhale, slowly pulling his fingers out. At that moment, I pushed him aside and ran out the door mumbling, "I'm sorry."

Chapter 3.

I don't know how I got through the next two days; I was in a feverish haze with my skin burning where Victor had touched me. Tonight was the night of the gala at the Parkview Palace. The city's biggest socialite event of the year. We were all required to assist with the gala, which was a relief as it would keep my mind occupied for the day. Maria and I went together to the Parkview Palace early in the morning. In the gala room, everything was buzzing. Event coordinators crossed tasks off their long lists, waiters set up the bar tables, and porters moved furniture and decorations around. All in perfectly orchestrated unison. I chuckled at the ant-like activity in the room. I walked up to Matt to get my directions for the night. He had divided the room into different service zones on a drawing, and he showed me my zone for tonight and gave me a list of the most important guests in that zone. I went over to a less busy corner to study the list, as I needed to be able to recognize and address the guests accordingly.

. . . .

THE BENEFIT GALA HAD the New York elite turning up in their most wonderful attire, and I was captivated by the atmosphere. I had my list of names and descriptions that I discreetly turned to once in a while as the guests simmered into the gala room. All of a sudden, I heard a recognizable voice behind me that made my skin tingle. I instinctively turned around to catch a glimpse of Victor. It seemed impossible to me, but he was even more attractive and magnetic in his navy-blue tuxedo. He was greeting his guests, laughing and conversing, with Ms. Perfect on his arm. She was truly impeccable. My stomach hurt, and I could feel a small sting in my heart. I redirected my focus to the guests within my zone, and put on a flirtatious and charming display as expected of me.

As I went around helping the guests find their tables, a sudden sensation made me turn. From across the room, Victor was watching me. I immediately looked away and pretended I hadn't seen him, but throughout the evening I could feel his gaze upon me.

ALL MY FIRSTS: PASSION AND HEARTACHE

Maybe I was overwhelmed with confusion from the sudden fire he had awoken in me, the discomfort of being watched so closely, or the realization that I was in over my head; in any case, I could feel my eyes water up. I withdrew to a dark corner to wipe my tears away, where no one would notice, when I could suddenly feel him close behind me. The warmth of his body on my arm, his scent, and the way my body reacted to his presence, revealed it was him without having to turn around.

"I know, she is a terrible speaker, but is she really that bad that you must cry," he whispered jestingly and nodded his head towards the old lady on the stage.

I had been too engrossed in my thoughts to notice that an elderly woman in a striking silver dress had taken the stage.

He continued, "I assure you, in a second, you will be out of your misery."

His lips were close to my ear, and I could feel his warm breath caressing my neck. As he whispered to me, the old lady raised her glass.

"See, I told you!" he said triumphantly. His joke had cheered me up, and I giggled. Everything about him, from his confidence and authority to his intense masculinity and erotic aura, mesmerized me and pulled me to him. Even his scent and voice had a hypnotizing effect on me. Someone called his name and waved at him, and he quickly put on his professional attitude. But before he walked away to talk to the person, he whispered to me, "Please meet me out on the terrace afterwards. We need to talk," and walked away.

As the gala event finally reached its end, and guests began to leave, I caught sight of Victor with flawless Elizabeth by his side saying goodnight to the guests. I disliked her. Anyone could look that well-groomed and elegant if they were born into money, I thought to myself, envy raving inside me. Victor had told me to meet him. Surely, he wanted to tell me to get over myself and that I had been a fun little distraction, but I had to move on now. I perfected his monologue inside my head, getting myself more and more worked up. If I stayed away, he would not get the pleasure. Leaving before they could leave me was my rule, and I would ensure that Victor wouldn't get there ahead of me. Instead of going out on the terrace, I found a quiet, dark room to gather my thoughts. I looked out at the skyline and felt lonely and lost.

"Are you hiding in here?" a voice behind me inquired.

He had found me. I closed my eyes and sighed, not ready for the conversation.

"No, of course not. I am just taking a few minutes before I head home," I said, trying to sound professional and hide the hurt inside. I felt so stupid.

"I was waiting for you on the terrace. Did you not hear me?" he said with a sharp tone.

I sighed. Leave him before he leaves you, a voice told me.

"I'm sorry, but we shouldn't have kissed. It was—"

"Wouldn't you say it was a bit more than a kiss?" he interrupted me. He looked at me teasingly, "I think I remember you moaning, when my fingers—"

I blushed and lost track of my thoughts for a moment. "It's not the point! We shouldn't. I'm sorry for my part. Let's put it behind us," I tried again.

There. We were done. It had all been a mistake. I brushed my clothes with my hands and walked with my head held high towards the door. Victor was leaning his back against the wall. He was looking at the ceiling.

As I was passing him on the way out, he looked at me.

"If this is what you want, I respect that. But honestly, I don't believe you."

He let his hand out, slowly reaching for mine. I stopped and looked down. I really didn't want to walk out, but I knew what the smart thing to do was. However, my heart and body wouldn't let me.

He could sense my hesitation. "There is something between us. Don't walk away like that. You torture me, and I feel like I'm chasing you around. Leonora," he paused and continued, "I don't like your games. But clearly you are still very young and have a lot to learn."

I raised my eyebrow, annoyed by his last comment.

"You are in a relationship. Maybe you don't have the morals to stay faithful, but I am not that type of girl."

He laughed at my insult and winked. "You already are that girl. It's too late to be remorseful." Big pause. He lowered his voice, "You are like no one, I have ever met. I can't figure out if I want to fuck you first or listen to you talk. I just know I want you," he said with a penetrating gaze.

Although I blushed out of awkwardness, I truly needed to hear such words. They wrapped around me like a passionate embrace. Nobody had ever expressed such a strong desire for me or talked to me like that. I didn't know what to answer. I was already in too deep.

"We shouldn't have...it was a mistake," I stuttered while trying to avoid his gaze.

"Don't run off again now," he said sternly. "It's a terrible habit of yours."

He moved slowly toward me. I could feel my legs getting weak. My heart was racing. My head was screaming for me to get out of here right now. To walk away while I still had a bit of dignity and an unbroken heart. I knew he was trouble. I knew this would not end well for me. I closed my eyes and let out a sigh as I gave in to my heart and body. Victor sensed my capitulation. Softly, he took my hand and led me out of the room. I followed like I was hypnotized. I could hear the buzzing noise of staff and guests, but it seemed so far, far away. All I could sense was Victor's grip of my hand, his intoxicating scent, and his breathing.

He led me to an elevator down the corridor. My head screamed for me to run away, yet I so desperately wanted to follow him. How did I end up with such intense conflicts raging within me? The doors closed behind us, and he let go of my hand. He looked at me and smiled before he brushed my hair gently to the side. Unexpectedly, he grabbed me by my waist and pulled me forcefully towards him. His lips and tongue took possession of mine, and I could hardly breathe with his passionate, strong kisses. He forced me against the elevator wall, pressing his body firmly against mine. He was rough. He took my hand and pressed it against his groin. It was hard, bulging, and growing with every second. Panic and excitement filled me.

I hadn't noticed the sound of the elevator coming to its floor, but Victor carried me out without stopping his passionate assault. He opened the door to the suite, and as we came in, he pushed me around so that he was behind me, kissing my neck roughly, with one hand around my throat and the other making its way up my skirt. He lifted up my skirt and made a satisfied noise, as he sensed my body was willing and ready for him. Everything was happening so quickly. Should I stop it now? I didn't want to. I so desperately yearned to feel a man like Victor inside me. Experience what a real man could do to me.

He led me to the master bedroom. He was not as rough now, but gentler, kissing me with deep kisses and caressing my body. He unbuttoned my shirt slowly and unzipped my skirt, all with great ease, so I was left in my underwear and stockings.

He smiled satisfiedly and whispered firmly, "Lie down."

I didn't move. I couldn't. He unbuttoned his shirt while I tried not to stare at his body, but I couldn't take my eyes off him. His body was as I had imagined; so muscular and firm that it looked like it had been carved out of stone with the inspiration of a Greek god. His body was perfect. As he unbuttoned his dark pants, he stood there with lust all over his face and his swollen erection pointing at me. It was long and thick, and precum was shining from the tip. He moved slowly toward me. I didn't know what he expected of me. He was looking hypnotized at my body, coming in closer, taking it all in. Never had I ever felt so unclothed.

He tossed me onto the bed. His erection was as hard as steel, his eyes were fixated on my small, perky breasts. It felt like he was breathing me in. He must have sensed my tension and nervousness.

"Just relax," he whispered in my ear, "I won't hurt you."

I breathed in and let out a big sigh, trying to relax. He lay down on me, kissing me slowly and gently from my neck down to my thighs. His finger caressed my inner thighs, teasing me. He began licking me carefully and tenderly between my legs, while his fingers were slowly making their way into me. Small shivers went through my body, as his tongue and fingers began moving quicker. I felt like crying out. My body was aching for him. He moved further up, and right then, I felt him penetrating me with a deep push. My eyes widened as a gasp escaped my lips. I looked up and into his eyes. His eyes were blurry from lust. His hands were all over me and made their way slowly down, reaching under my buttocks and lifting them up while squeezing my cheeks tight. He was heavy on me, and the way he had forced his way inside me, created a strong throbbing sensation joined with overwhelming pleasure that made me whimper. I wanted to feel him so badly, have him fill me up, and never have him stop, while my head was going crazy with thoughts. My whimpers and moans seemed to intensify his desire as he pounded harder and harder now, pinning my wrists down to the bed. The musky scent of his body was invading my thoughts, making everything foggy. I could feel tingles in my toes making their way up through every fiber in my body. An overwhelming tension built up inside me. Each muscle inside me seemed to contract. I struggled to breathe and let out an involuntary, loud moan as an explosion of complete pleasure filled my entire body. His pace went quicker and quicker. He let out a loud grunt, his body trembling, and I could feel his release inside me and the warm semen filling me up. He kissed my neck, closed his eyes, and smiled. He didn't pull out of me or roll to the side. He stayed inside me, kissing me tenderly. Small contractions inside me continued to squeeze around him and make him groan each time.

He whispered, barely audible in my ear, "I'm so glad you changed your mind."

We lay there for a few minutes, in an intimate embrace, with him still inside me. His phone rang, and he gently pulled out of me and got up. He left me with a full view of his perfectly shaped back and bottom as he walked out of the room. I felt self-conscious as I lay there in the big, empty bed. I blushed at the thought of what had just happened and pulled the duvet over me, while I looked for my underwear. The intense tingling sensation continued, traveling up and down my body, and I could feel him inside me still. Excitement and awkwardness overwhelmed me. It was unlike anything I had ever experienced before. To be taken like that, firmly yet gently. And not by any man; a man like Victor. I put on my underwear, hurried into the bathroom and grabbed a bathrobe. I contemplated taking a shower, but I didn't have any clean clothes to put on.

I stayed in the bathroom for maybe 10 minutes. I didn't know what else to do with myself. His business call must have finished as he called my name. I opened the bathroom door and went back to the bedroom. He sat on the bed, still naked, with his phone in his hand. He got up and walked slowly towards me with a rapacious look.

He whispered in my ear, "I want to hear you moan like that again. Just louder this time."

I went crimson red and looked down. The way, he had made my body involuntary explode in pleasure, was an overwhelming new feeling to me, and now he was shamelessly talking about it. He could sense my reluctance.

"Was it your first?" he asked, not able to hide his contentment.

I felt so embarrassed now. Why were we talking about this? I wanted him to think of me as a sexy, experienced lover, and he obviously saw right through me.

He opened my bathrobe, put his hands around my waist, and kissed me tenderly. Our tongues played teasingly and slowly. He lifted me up and carefully put me down on the big bed. He began kissing me softly all over my body, once again moving slowly down from my neck to my inner thighs, taking his time. His fingers played with me gently, sending electric shocks through my body each time they moved to a new spot. He was so gentle. He moved his lips back up to my nipples, and his tongue played and teased me slowly, while his hands were carefully gliding up and down my thighs. He was careful not to let his fingers slip inside me, although I was yearning for him to do so. He was going to let me wait this time. Every fiber and hair on my body was electric from his touches, and I could feel how wet I was. Finally, he slowly moved his head down between my legs and began licking me. I couldn't take it anymore, and I tried to pull him up towards me.

"Say it!" he commanded.

I wasn't a dirty talker, but he was driving me crazy from lust and anticipation.

"Take me. Now," I moaned.

He curled his lips in satisfaction. He moved up and kissed me deeply, while our eyes were locked. Without taking his eyes off me and still kissing me intensely, he slowly, bit by bit got inside me. I gasped in between our kisses.

"You are so incredibly tight. Like nothing I have ever felt," he whispered.

He continued kissing me so deeply, passionately, yet slowly. His movements were unhurried and gentle, and he was pulling in and out of me gently in rhythm to our kisses. I felt like exploding.

I have had one-night stands and boyfriends, but I had never ever felt so physically close and intimate with someone before. Having him slowly move in and out of me while gazing into my eyes and kissing me was beyond my wildest fantasy. I could hear his breathing change as he tried to control himself. He lifted my bottom to get me into the right angle, and I could feel how he felt so different inside me now. He pounded slowly on a spot that made my eyes water while leaving me breathless. He bit my neck and thrust more rapidly now. He put his hand on my throat, which made it harder for me to breathe. And then. An explosion of unbelievable pleasure flooded me and took over all my senses, making me unable to see or breathe for a moment. The distant sound of a scream reached my ears, and I recognized it as coming from me. Victor moaned loudly and rolled over to the side. I lay there, unable to move, panting while an unfamiliar, peaceful wave rolled over me.

"Forget what the young boys have tried with you. This is what it should be like."

· · · ·

I WOKE UP FEELING HIS hands cupping my breasts, biting my neck, and breathing heavily into my ruffled hair. He was pressing his body firmly against mine from behind. I could feel he was highly aroused and ready for more. He spread my legs, pulled my buttocks firmly toward him, and once again had me moan uncontrollably in ecstasy. I fell in and out of sleep that night, being woken again and again by him. He didn't seem to be able to get enough. I think I counted four or five times more. At 4 a.m. in the morning, his thirst for me seemed to have been clenched. I tried to fall asleep, but I was too sore to find rest. My lips were bruised, my nipples hurt, and I felt ravaged inside. I don't know when, but eventually I fell asleep. Not for long, though, as he woke me up already at 5 a.m.

"I have to take you back to Imperial Towers before everyone gets up."

I put on yesterday's underwear and uniform, tried to brush my hair with my fingers, and did a sleepy walk of shame over to the elevator. Victor was already dressed. His suit was messy and his hair ruffled, but he still looked amazing. The elevator took us down to the underground parking garage. He led me over to the black Audi and opened the door for me. He seemed deep in thought, and I was barely awake. New York City hadn't woken up just yet either, so we had the streets almost to ourselves and arrived quickly at the Imperial Towers. As we drove down the ramp to the parking garage, Victor put his hand on my thigh.

"You're off at 5 p.m., right? Come to the penthouse," he said, looking over at me.

I smiled and nodded. Right here and now, I felt complete. Realistically, there would never be a happy ending to this, but in this moment, I was unable to complete those thoughts. He parked the car, got out, and opened my door.

"See you tonight," he said.

I hurried over to the exit and unlocked the door leading into the staircase to the staff quarters. I made it back to my room without anyone seeing me.

· · · ·

THE REST OF THE DAY passed in a feverish haze. All I could think about were the passionate kisses, his touches, the pleasurable pain of penetration, his dominance, and the overwhelming sensations that had made me scream uncontrollably. Lust had taken over my mind, and I was relieved when the clock was finally getting close to 5 p.m.

Maria nudged me. "Why are you so tired today? You are barely here."

Just then, Victor and Phillip came out of the elevator and passed us on their way out on the terrace, and nodded towards Maria and me. I tried to hide the grin that instinctively played on my lips.

"My day just got better," she said jokingly. I had to agree with her. "I think Phillip is starting to take over as president," she continued.

Finally, the clock turned 5 p.m. I hurried down to my room, showered, shaved my legs, and washed my hair. I dabbed on some perfume and put lotion on my body. I found a set of black lacey underwear to put on, and for lack of anything else, I decided on a green casual dress with white spots. I put on makeup and looked at myself. I was happy with my look. Ready to see Victor, I walked determinedly to the staircase. I went to the 5th floor, took the elevator to the 10th floor, and then took the stairs to the final floors. I didn't want to risk being caught.

I knocked on the door to the penthouse. Almost as if, he had waited for me behind the door, he opened it immediately. He pulled me inside and closed the door behind me.

"You have tortured my mind all day," he said. "I haven't been able to think of anything, but you. I might have fucked you once or twice too much last night, I am so sore. But I need you right now. I can't think of anything else," he said before grabbing me by my waist.

He pushed me up against the wall, and I leaned back, surrendering myself completely to his desire. This time, it was all for him. He turned me around, cupped my breasts aggressively, and pushed my legs apart with his own legs. I could feel him push himself inside me, and I closed my eyes in pain. I too was sore, yet it felt breathtakingly satisfying.

"Are you okay?" he grunted, but absolute electrifying pleasure made me unable to talk. He finished almost as quickly as he had started. I could feel semen dripping out of me. He grinned as he pulled his pants up and handed me a cloth.

¨ ′"Sorry for the assault. I will make it up for you later, I promise."

I pulled my dress down and wiped my thighs, feeling suddenly very self-conscious. He must have sensed my uneasiness, so he took the cloth from me and gently wiped my thighs.

"Now where are my manners!" he said with a reassuring smile at me.

I certainly needed him to reassure me, because he had led me down a bewildering path, I had never traveled before. I was 21 years old, raised in a very conservative and prudish family, and here I was—entirely sober even—engaged in unimaginable passionate sex with a man 10 years older. A man so experienced and sensual. Victor. A man I didn't really know. I felt nauseous. The urge to come up with an excuse and leave surged strongly within me. But before, I could fabricate an excuse, he took my hand and led me out on the terrace.

The large ball lamps on the terrace floor created a soft and warm glow against the dark purple sky of the city. It was beautiful and peaceful, and I could feel myself getting more relaxed.

"Come let's sit on the couch," he said pointing to the corner couch.

I sat down at the furthest end of the couch with my knees to my chest. He poured me a glass of champagne and himself a glass of whiskey, then sat down next to me.

"Let me know if I should get you some cushions to help you build a fortress?" he said teasingly.

"Leonora, I know what you taste like and how you moan in pleasure, so let's skip over this sudden shyness."

He really had a way of making me feel like a silly, insecure girl.

"I thought you might be hungry, so I took the liberty of ordering dinner on your behalf," he said and pointed to a table set up with wine and dinner.

"Vegan, of course," he smiled.

Dinner was amazing, and except for the first few minutes of quiet awkwardness when the champagne hadn't yet calmed me entirely, we talked and laughed all through dinner. He told me about his ambitions for the hotel chain, and I shared details about my work and life at the previous hotels. We talked about how different the Danish educational system was to the American, and he was impressed with the fact, that Latin and ancient history were obligatory classes in high school, and my class had been on study trips to

Germany, France, and Italy. We talked about so many different things, but we didn't touch on sensitive subjects like the situation surrounding us.

After dinner, I was sleepy from the wine and lack of sleep, and I tried to suppress a yawn, but Victor noticed.

He laughed. "I'm tired too. Something kept me up all night."

I didn't know what was expected of me at this point in the evening. Was I expected to leave? I desperately wanted to sleep, but I didn't want to break this magical moment and leave him.

"I really enjoyed talking to you," he said and began kissing my neck.

"I would love for you to stay the night, but honestly, it would kill me to be so close to you and unable to fuck you as much as I want," he said, biting my neck to emphasize his words, and whispered then teasingly in my ear, "You are so tight, I could barely walk today. I will find you tomorrow."

Chapter 4.

The following weeks were weird and wonderful. I was sore and bruised from the intense and passionate encounters we had on every possible occasion. Victor had a ferocious hunger for me that I was more than willing to give in to. At night, I couldn't find rest either. Vivid dreams of his hands on my body, his fingers teasing and caressing me, his lips on my nipples, our devouring kisses, and the unimaginable pleasure he offered me again and again, interrupted my sleep. During the day, I was distracted as my mind continuously went back to the heated encounters. Our secret put a glow on my cheeks and a cheeky smile on my lips that were difficult to hide. I had never been taken like that. Never felt a man touch me so possessively and greedily. He knew what he wanted and how, there was no fiddling or fumbling. Just unadulterated desire.

This late afternoon, Matt had gone home for the day, Damian and Simon were servicing guests in their rooms, and the lounge and library were occupied by the usual businessmen networking and discussing projects keeping Leon and Maria busy, and I worked on my projects in my office. Suddenly, I heard the office door close behind me and the lock turn. The tiny hairs on the back of my neck tingled, as a wave of anticipation washed over me. With a firm grasp, Victor pulled me from my chair, and without saying any words, he skillfully propelled me right into a state of craving that only he could fulfill. He was more than eager to help me reach my climax, and I released a long and deep moan, my body trembling against his. As I sat on his lap afterwards, he caressed my thigh.

"I'm meeting Elizabeth for drinks later today in the lounge. Just so you are prepared."

"Sure," I shrugged indignantly, but inside my heart was burning and my stomach turned upside down.

He began to kiss and tickle the small hairs on my neck. I wanted to push him away and get up, but I didn't want him to see how hurt I was. What a fool I was! I felt disgusted by myself. I had his semen inside me right at this moment, and he was planning a date night with his girlfriend.

"You are comparing apples and oranges in your head right now," he said. "This is simple and fun, let's keep it this way. All that matters is right here and now."

Apparently, I wasn't as skilled an actress as I thought, as Victor had seen right through my act.

Although Victor so graciously gave me a heads-up so I could keep away, neither this nor the warning voice inside me could stop me. I was drawn to the lounge like a moth to a flame. A moth to a bug zapper lamp. I found an excuse to work behind the bar, and eventually, they arrived together looking perfect in all their radiating splendor. Was the sex with her as rough and passionate? It was hard to imagine someone so classy and flawless actually having sex, and even more impossible to imagine it with someone as erotic and intense as Victor. As if he could read my mind, Victor looked over at me, and a small, dirty smile played on his lips for the few seconds, he looked at me.

• • • •

I DON'T KNOW HOW I had managed to finish the final touches to the competitor analysis because my mind had been all over the place these past weeks. I was quite pleased with my work and my recommendations for improvements for the Elite and VIP services. Matt too was so impressed that he wanted me to present it myself at the management meeting. I didn't like to do presentations. I used to stay home those days I had to give presentations at school. Matt wouldn't let me out of it, but promised he would support me in any way during the presentation. I had a few days to prepare my analysis, and I actually stayed away from Victor to concentrate myself fully on the task.

• • • •

FINALLY, THE DAY ARRIVED and I was looking forward to get it over with. I was already nervous, and of course, Victor then had to place himself next to me, which got everyone confused trying to find out how they should seat themselves in accordance. I presented my analysis and my suggestions to the management, and everyone smiled and were pleased with my work. I answered questions from the management, and afterwards they went on to discuss my suggestions.

"I will reward you later," Victor whispered to me, and squeezed my thigh under the table.

I could feel Matt's observant gaze on me.

Later that day, Victor walked past me discreetly and signaled for me to follow him into a corner.

"You did a great job today. But I knew you would. Matt will discuss with you how we proceed. That's not what I want to talk to you about. You and I are going away. I have told Matt that you are needed at the Parkview Palace tonight and tomorrow. Where do you want to go?"

I was taken aback by the invitation. I hadn't expected it.

"You don't need to decide right now, but I need to know within the next hour. I'll be at my office," he said and walked away.

I looked confused as he walked away. But I had plenty of places on my bucket list, and although they probably weren't what he was expecting, I didn't want to miss a chance to go there. I went down to his office.

"Badlands National Park in South Dakota, please," I said with a big smile on my face.

He looked at me with surprise.

"I have never heard about that place!" he laughed. "Okay, fine. It's not what I was expecting, but nothing about you is. Meet me in the parking garage in two hours, okay?"

. . . .

I HAD PACKED A SMALL bag with clothes and was waiting for Victor in the parking garage. He came out of the elevator a few minutes later, while shaking his head in disbelief.

"Next time, do a bit of research before you decide on a place. There aren't even any direct flights to the airport from here," he grinned.

I looked at him with disappointment, "Are you serious? I have no idea where it actually is. It just looked nice."

"It's fine, I promised to take you there, and I will."

He opened the door for me, and I got in. This time, sitting in his car felt much better than the first time.

"Next stop: the airport," he said, accelerating out of the garage.

At JFK Airport, a private plane was waiting for us. He led me into the plane, where a sweet stewardess greeted us with a glass of champagne each. The pilot came out to say hello and inform us about the weather and length of the flight. As the plane took off, Victor raised his glass.

"Cheers for the world's least discreet getaway trip," he laughed.

I felt so bad about having him charter a private plane for us. That had never been my intention.

"You had my assistant almost in tears, I think," he continued, "Finding somewhere decent to stay in or near the national park wasn't easy either, but he managed."

He moved from the seat across from me and sat down next to me. We kissed almost throughout the entire flight, only broken off by his business calls and some emails once in a while.

We landed in Rapid City in the late hours of the afternoon, where a rental Jeep waited for us.

"I gathered you probably wanted to stay inside the national park. The only accommodation available are simple cabins. I can take you there, or I can take you to a hotel outside the park."

I smiled at him.

"Now that you have gone through all this trouble, we should stay inside the national park."

We drove through a landscape with dramatic rock formations, vast open spaces, and strikingly barren yet beautiful views. We made a stop at the White River Valley Overlook just as the sun was going down, to watch the rock formations showcase an incredible array of deep red and orange hues that was absolutely spectacular. As we drove further in, small quaint and rustic log cabins were spread out over the area, blending beautifully in with the breathtaking natural surroundings, and as we pulled up to our small rustic log cabin, Victor looked over at me while shaking his head bemused. He opened the door to the log cabin and carried my bag inside. It was simple and cozy inside. Only the bare necessities, but enough to make you comfortable and forget the hectic world outside the national park.

"I can go get us something to eat from the restaurant in a bit," he said, pulling me down on the soft bed with him. "But first, let us see if the beds live up to our standards," he said and began to undress me. I pushed him down and took over. I placed myself on top of him, undressed my blouse, and put his hands on my breasts. Then I unbuttoned his shirt while I kissed his nipples and let my fingers run over his chest and slowly down to his belly button. I opened his belt and gradually unzipped his pants, letting his erection come out in full view. Hungrily, I licked the tip while my hand gripped hard at the root. He moaned as I eagerly moved my head up and down to take him in as much as I could. He adjusted himself and moved my hair to the side so he could watch me go down on him.

"Don't stop now," he groaned, and put his hands in a tight grip around my head as he released himself in my mouth.

He trembled uncontrollably.

"You dirty little girl. I didn't know you were into this. Now, I know how to keep you full."

He winked at me as he pulled me down to his side.

We lay there for a while, until he got dressed and went over to the restaurant to get us something to eat.

We sat outside on the handcrafted pine deck chairs on the veranda with our burgers. The night sky was black and sprinkled with stars. Everything was so quiet and peaceful. Sometimes, the sound of wildlife could be heard in the distance.

I pointed to the sky. "There is the Big Dipper. I think that's what you call it here, right?"

Victor looked up at the stars. "You know, I was born and raised in the city, I don't think I have ever gazed at the stars, let alone known their names."

I pointed out the constellations to him, that I knew, and we sat quietly in the dark for an hour just looking at the stars, satellites, and airplanes. It was absolutely magical. When it was time to go to bed, he lifted me up and carried me inside.

"Leonora," he whispered in the dark, "promise me, we keep it simple like this."

"Of course," I whispered absent-mindedly, as he sucked on my nipples and already had his fingers teasing me between my legs.

I woke up in the middle of the night and couldn't fall back to sleep.

"Are you awake?" I whispered.

Victor turned on the night lamp by his side of the bed.

"I can't sleep either. Do you want to sit outside on the veranda?"

We wrapped the quilts around us and went outside to sit in the dark.

"How many boyfriends have you had?" he asked out of a sudden.

"Ehm, two," I answered hesitantly.

"How many guys have you slept with?" he continued.

"Why?" I felt uncomfortable. "I'm not even sure it's okay to ask a girl that," I answered.

"It's okay. I'm just curious about you".

Seven or eight, I answered silently in my head. I had been a late bloomer. I had dated and kissed many guys, before I moved to England, but I had never had an actual boyfriend or had sex, before I met Sven, a South African sous chef. He had been my first boyfriend, my first love, followed by Ian, another chef, this time English. I had had some casual one-night stands after Ian. Now that I felt Victor's intense desire for me, I realized with regret that whatever I thought I had before was insignificant.

"Why do you cheat?" I asked him back in return.

He looked at me for a while, studying my face intently.

"If I didn't, I wouldn't be here in the Badlands for the first time. With you," he smiled avoiding the question. "But I was actually the one asking questions. You can have your turn, when I'm done," he said grinning. "Why did you leave Denmark? You were what, 18 years old?"

I took a deep breath and thought about it a bit, before I answered. "I wanted more out of life, I guess. To get away from everything. It was a strong impulse, I had to follow, and when I saw a job advert for a hotel job in England, I applied and got the job over the phone a few days later. That's it."

"That's it. You are very impulsive. How did your parents react?" he asked inquisitively.

I told him a bit about my parents and how I had always been impulsive, so they weren't surprised at all, when I left. Victor, on the other hand, told me about growing up in New York and about his role in the family. We talked for two hours under the starry night sky, until the cold made us go back to bed. I fell asleep with my head inside his armpit, enwrapped in his scent.

. . . .

THE NEXT MORNING, I woke up to the smell of coffee. Victor was in the kitchen area, with just boxer shorts on, making coffee and toast. He noticed I was awake and came over to me. "Finally! You missed the sunrise. I thought you were going to sleep the entire day."

I looked at the clock on the wall; it was 8.30. I made a grimace and got up.

"I can't get proper reception here, and I have just one call, I need to make this morning. So, I'm sorry, we need to go to the nearest town."

The drive was 20 minutes across the Badlands Wall, which revealed out-of-this-world views of the Badlands and prairie scenery. I counted 15 bison, before we pulled into an empty parking lot.

"It won't take long, I promise," he said and made the call.

Our definition of time was surely conflicting. For more than 30 minutes, Victor discussed diversification strategies, investment risk, assets, and similar matters with what sounded like two men, on the other end of the line. While he was getting deeply engrossed in equity securities and defensive stocks, I was getting more and more bored sitting here listening to half of it. I studied Victor while he was occupied. He exuded a blend of confidence and focused determination. Even when speaking on the phone, his ability to command attention was unmistakable. His ability to actually listen and take in opinions was evident in the occasional pauses he took, yet there was no doubt that he was in control of the conversation.

The conversation finally sounded as if it was coming to an end. Victor was clearly pleased with the outcome and diverted his attention shortly to me, while still on the phone. He looked at me mischievously and placed my hand firmly on his groin, as he leaned his seat back and opened his pants. I smiled at him teasingly, kissed his cheek, and moved my head slowly down to taste him. I thought he would finish the meeting, but out of the blue, he changed the topic to an exit strategy for a specific company, he wanted to cut ties with. By the sound of it, the two men were not happy about the suggestion and sounded shocked. Victor remained steadfast; he wouldn't yield on this issue, and I could feel how he tensed up and became aggravated. I gave up and got back in my seat and watched him. He quickly dismissed the men, telling them to find a solution, and finished the call. He took some deep breaths after he hung up, and then leaned over to kiss me.

"Let's try again without the diversion," he said.

I moved slowly towards him again; I devoured him, tasted him, and teased him. It was hard for him to not take control of my pace and depth, but I softly bit him each time he tried to, and eventually he gave in and let me do as I pleased with him.

As I swallowed, he squeezed my thigh and joked, "If this is what the weather here does to you, we should come here more often."

We drove back into the national park and made a stop at the different hiking trails. We walked among an abundance of colorful flowers and even found a few small seashell fossils, much to my delight. We held hands during our hikes and continued our conversation from the night before. Victor told me about his brothers. I wanted to ask about Elizabeth, as the thought of her grew stronger each day. But I couldn't.

We finished our drive around the park and returned to our cabin.

"We have the cottage until the morning. Let's get the best out of it before we leave tonight."

He opened the passenger seat for me and opened the door to the log cabin. He took my hand and led me to the bathroom, where he undressed me quickly before pulling me into the small shower with him. While water poured down on our bodies, we kissed and caressed each other. He wrapped my legs around his hips and positioned me against the wall. Everything Victor ever did with me was executed with skill and determination; each move was clearly perfected through practice. Although his erotic confidence was a huge turn-on for me and obviously the reason why he could take me to such heights of pleasure, which no guy had been capable of before, I also wished it wasn't a constant reminder of the endless number of women before me. He pulled me out of my thoughts, as he pushed himself inside me and spellbound me with long, deep kisses. Just as I was about to feel my body explode, he pulled out of me, leaving me gasping and deeply frustrated.

"Shh, we are not done yet."

He lifted me up and carried me over to the bed. He placed himself behind me and let his fingers run slowly down my back until they reached my butt cheeks. He gently pushed them to the side and let his thumb deliberately glide inside me, gently massaging me.

"Is it okay?" he breathed softly.

I nodded. He got up, found some oil in the kitchen, and went back to the bed.

"Try to relax as much as you can now," he said, before he slowly, bit by bit, slid inside me. For each gentle push, he groaned loudly, and I gasped, clutching the sheets. I whimpered. The feeling was overwhelming and intense. He moved his hand in between my legs to tease and taunt me further. Suddenly, the discomfort changed into complete pleasure, sending shocks through my body, and I gasped for breath as if I were choking. I screamed out as the contractions inside me hit every nerve in my body like napalm. My entire body felt like it was struck by lightning. My senses were on overdrive. But Victor wasn't done.

He guided me down on my back and commanded, "Play with yourself," while he quickly cleaned himself with a cloth, and then placed himself over me and took me again, thrusting me hard as he lifted my hips up. Harder and quicker, he thrusted, until we moaned out in unison, trembling against each other. Sweaty and panting, we lay there.

How many more tricks did he have up his sleeve?

"Are you okay?" he asked softly when I hadn't said anything for a while.

I nodded. I felt like crying. Why was he my first in everything? He would leave me with nothing when this was over. I felt completely vulnerable with him. Exposed. Victor cuddled me, as if he could feel I wasn't okay. His caring embrace made me cry, and I let myself give into all the tears. He held me for half an hour without any of us speaking.

"Would you like to talk about it?" he asked tenderly.

"I'm fine. It's fine. It's just a strange situation between us. And I am fine with this, but it just got too much."

"I know. We will not do that again, if our situation makes it difficult for you. I never knew someone like you existed, and I don't ever want to see you hurt".

We flew home, and Victor dropped me off at the Imperial Towers before he pulled me in and passionately kissed me goodnight.

"I will be gone for a few days. I have business meetings in Dubai. Be a good girl until I am back," he said before he drove off again.

Back in my room, I changed into a nightdress and got comfortable in my bed with one of the books I had borrowed from the hotel library. I read a few pages before falling asleep.

• • • •

MY ALARM CLOCK WOKE me up much too early. I dragged myself out of bed to go work out. The Badlands had been absolutely beautiful, and being with Victor outside of work had been equally unique. Laughter, flirtatious banter, and meaningful conversations had brought us closer. I was deeply fascinated by him, his masculinity and confidence, his intellect, how he was both possessive and attentive, and, of course, the flame he had lit inside me. Actually, I was more than fascinated. I liked him. Not butterflies-in-my-stomach liked him. It was a stronger feeling that I could not explain. And yet, my heart ached. I don't know how I ever fooled myself into believing I could do this. Maybe the feverish yearning for him had muddled my mind to the point where I hadn't realized how far down the dark path, I had actually gone. Victor had made it perfectly clear about his intentions. Several times. His words echoed in my mind. It all brought back memories, I had tried to bury. My first boyfriend had been Sven. I had just moved to England, when he laid his eyes on me. He was the 10-year older sous chef, and I was a waitress. He got me in sight and cornered me, and I thought it was love. But only when I was in too deep, daydreaming about marriage and kids, did I realize that I was just a casual fling before he headed back to South Africa. It hurt even more when I discovered everybody else had known. Unlike Sven, Victor had been very frank about not being interested in more than sex with me, so I was even more of a fool this time. I took some deep breaths and went upstairs to work.

"Leonora," Damian sneaked up on me. "Are you going up? I have something to show you."

Always there to make me smile. We got into the elevator, and I looked amused at him.

"Wait, you will be blown away this time," he said looking dramatic.

Between the 4th and 5th floor, he hit the elevator door hard, and the elevator stopped. He pulled the doors aside, revealing a wall shelf with a bundle of keys and a black keycard. "Now you may not be impressed just yet, but wait until I tell you, that I now have access to every room and cabinet in the hotel," he exclaimed.

I laughed.

He smiled at me, "So, is it time for me to dump my girlfriend?"

"Almost yes!" I giggled. "But what in the world should we do with the keys?" I asked.

"Well, I know how you have been dreaming about the bathrobes. Now is your time to get yourself a warm and fluffy bathrobe with a golden logo on. And you don't even have to sleep with that old creepy dude from housekeeping!" he jested. "We will pick you up at midnight."

· · · ·

MATT WAS ALREADY IN the office, when I came in. "How was Parkview Palace?" he asked. I had prepared some lies, and thankfully he didn't ask more questions. Instead, he turned his attention to a big pile of paperwork.

"So, management loved you and your work on the analysis. You have moved up the ladder, my dear," he smiled. "You will take on a greater responsibility and more strategic work, and I will get someone else to assist with the direct contact with the guests. Are you happy?"

I was surprised, but yes, also happy. I smiled at him and sat down at my desk. I could still feel Victor's burning touch on my body. He was like a drug to me. Temporary ecstasy that always led to feverish withdrawal.

Eventually, the day passed, and right before midnight, there was a quiet knock on the door. I had already put on a jumper and some sweatpants, so I got quickly out of bed and opened the door. Simon and Damian were standing outside. They had their uniforms on.

"Was I supposed to have a uniform on?" I asked.

"Nah, you'll probably be okay if we get caught."

We took the stairs to the 18th floor and tiptoed down the corridor. There was a discreetly hidden door that Damian pointed to.

"How do you know?" I asked.

Simon smiled and winked, "I had a good chat with Maria or Marla or whatever in housekeeping."

Damian took out the bundle of keys and went through each one of them. Finally, the door clicked, and we hurried inside. Inside, the softest bathrobes hang on one side of the wall. We quickly took one each, wrapped it around us, and looked around for more stuff. Then Simon lifted three bottles of white wine up high with a beaming smile.

"I can't find glasses, so it will just be a bottle each."

We sat down on the floor in our fluffy bathrobes, had warm white wine, and joked and laughed so much that my stomach ached. Eventually, we tiptoed back down in our new bathrobes.

. . . .

A FEW DAYS LATER, I could hear Victor and Phillip come down the corridor. My heart skipped a beat, and I could feel a sense of relief and comfort wash over me. They came into the office to say good morning to us. Victor was back from Dubai looking magnetic and gorgeous as always, although I tried to avoid looking at him. If I looked at him, my secret would have been revealed. We small-talked politely, all four of us, before they went to their meeting.

But just before Victor walked out, he casually said, "Gary from Parkview sends his wishes; he was very pleased with you."

I didn't look up, but pretended to be busy with my notebook.

. . . .

AUTUMN WAS TRANSFORMING New York into a captivating tableau of rich and warm hues. The air carried a brisk yet invigorating chill, while the city transitioned from the vibrant energy of summer to the contemplative embrace of winter. With the change of season, the upcoming management dinner was almost here. Apparently, each quarter, management and the board went out for dinner. I wasn't actually part of management, even if I had moved up the ranks. Unexpectedly, I was added to the mailing list today. Matt didn't raise an eyebrow, but then again, he wouldn't have made it to where he was, if he wasn't discreet and kept assumptions to himself.

Inexperienced with the management dinners, I didn't know what was expected of me. I borrowed a black dress from Maria, and she helped me do a wavy two-bun updo that really complimented my face. I carefully put on formal makeup, and Maria pretended to give a standing ovation, when I was ready to leave.

I shared a taxi with Matt and our HR director to Eleven Madison Park. I wasn't a food enthusiast, but even I had heard great things about Eleven Madison Park as a high-end, extraordinary gastronomic experience. I was both excited and nervous about joining the heads of the company in such a world-renowned restaurant.

Tonight, Victor didn't seem to care too much if anyone caught on to us. The second he saw us enter the room, he left a conversation and walked over to accompany me to a chair at the table to put my bag.

"Come sit here next to me. You will sit at the kids' table tonight," he said nodding jestingly towards Phillip and Arthur.

With his hand on my back, he walked around, introducing me to everyone, except for the two older men. One was Mr. Oppenheim, and the other, I learned, was Mr. Phillips, an important business partner and stakeholder. Except for a few odd stares from Mr. Phillips throughout the night, if anyone else wondered why I was there, they politely concealed their thoughts. I had a great evening, and the kids' table was the perfect place for me. I was thankful for Victor to have seated me between him and Phillip, even if, from the outside, it seemed like an inappropriate seat for a girl in my position at a management dinner.

To avoid drawing too much attention to Victor and myself, I mostly talked to Phillip. He reminded me somehow of Damian, and I giggled so much in his company that Victor gave him a short reprimand a few times, instructing him to tone it down a bit. Although it wasn't the place for intimate conversation or gestures, Victor still made sure I felt comfortable. He held my hand discreetly under the table and ensured I was included in every conversation. He was, as always, attentive, and I felt so protected and content sitting here next to him. Even if Victor wasn't my boyfriend and even if he didn't want me as much as he wanted Elizabeth, he was more caring and attentive to me than anyone had ever been. Having an affair with Victor was the best thing that had happened in my life, yet it was also one of my worst decisions. It was slowly destroying me to be so deeply intimate and exposed with someone, who I felt rejected by every day for not being his chosen. As dinner was slowly coming to an end, Victor whispered in my ear to wait for him outside the restaurant.

It was rainy and cold outside, and it took a while before he came out. Both Phillip and Matt came over to ask if I needed help to get home, but I assured them I was fine and was just waiting for my Uber. Finally, Victor came out. He was engaged in a heated conversation with his father. They were subtle and discreet, so I couldn't hear the words, but it was an issue that was obviously aggravating Victor. Without even trying to be discreet in front of his father, he walked over to me, put his hand around my waist, led me to his car, and opened the door for me.

• • • •

THAT NIGHT, HE DIDN'T take me back to the Imperial Towers. He drove me somewhere else. "I do have a home. I don't always live in hotels, you know," he said with a playful smile.

I was actually surprised. Somehow, I had never considered that he could have a home outside the Imperial or Parkview. He drove us to Park Avenue and parked outside a building with a grand façade, adorned with architectural elegance. He greeted the doorman, and they exchanged a few words quietly.

He led me to his apartment, which was just as I would imagine a man like him would live: a panorama of Manhattan's iconic skyline through floor-to-ceiling windows, artwork displayed on the walls, a large fireplace, and large black leather sofas. The living room was adjoined to a perfectly decorated office, that had piles of papers and books everywhere. It wasn't as tidy as a hotel suite; this was his home. It felt special and privileged to have been invited in.

"I like it," I said. "Next time, let me show you my place," I laughed.

He kissed my neck while walking right behind me, showing me the different rooms. As we passed a shelf with picture frames, he swiftly put one of them down. He hadn't been discreet enough, and I knew exactly what and who he was trying to hide.

"It doesn't matter," he whispered in my ear. "You and I are here right now, that is what matters."

But it didn't feel like that was all that mattered. He cheated on her. Did he cheat on me? With her, most likely. But with others as well?

"Come," he said leading me to his bedroom.

There were no curtains; we were surrounded by the skyline. That night, we made love that was so tender and slow. I felt happy. I kissed him goodnight and snuggled into his armpit to fall asleep enwrapped in his scent.

Victor fell quickly asleep, but his buzzing mobile kept waking me up. I leaned over him to turn on the night lamp, but as I did, I accidentally knocked his mobile to the floor. It lit up, and I could see 10 missed calls from 'Maya X' on the screen. I picked the mobile up, and right then a text message appeared. 'Babe?' it said. I froze. I felt a cold sweat roll over me. I got up. Impulsively, I went over to his nightstand and opened the drawer to look for more cues. Condoms?! He had never used a condom with me! Did he use a condom with Elizabeth? I didn't want to imagine them having sex, but if I did, using a condom with her and not with me seemed too strange. Was it a third woman? Or a fourth or fifth—what did I know?! And she was invited into his bedroom, which I had only just been now. I felt sick. The joke was on me. I felt enraged. Tears ran uncontrollably down my cheeks. My heart was aching. I had longed for so long for someone to love me and make me feel taken care of, and Victor had been the only one to show me that kind of affection and attention. Victor, who also made it quite clear that he wasn't interested in more than casual sex. He had led me into a completely unknown world, with uncontrollable moans and screams, trembles, limitless pleasure, and an all-consuming desire that drove me crazy day and night. He had woken a side of me that I had never known existed until he touched me the first time, and the fear that I might never experience and feel this way again with someone else was breaking me. And now, I painfully realized that to him, this wasn't even unique; I was nothing special. He gave me everything I yearned for, but at the same time, he withheld it. I felt so lost. Every first time with him robbed me of the chance to share the first time with someone who would actually care.

An intense anger ignited within me. I went straight for the kill. I woke him up.

"Maya wants to talk to you!"

He looked confused as he tried to wake up and understand the situation.

I pointed to his phone. "Maya wants to talk. Are you not going to call her back? I think she misses her 'babe.'"

He picked up his phone and saw the missed calls and the text message. He sighed, threw the phone down, and reached out for me, but I avoided him. He didn't say anything, but I didn't care.

"I think you should call her. Now. Tell her that the drawer is stocked with condoms, so you are all ready for her!"

He looked over at the drawer.

"Why did you never have the courtesy to wear a condom with me?" I screamed.

"We don't need to wear a condom," he said calmly.

I felt sick to my stomach.

"Is it Elizabeth or someone else? No, actually I don't care about who you sleep with!"

I did care. I sobbed.

"Condoms are a sign of respect, and then I find out you are actually more than happy to use them. It's just me you have no respect for. Which is fine, I should have known. You make me feel like a prostitute. No less than that, because I don't even get paid."

Rage filled me up again.

"Fuck it, I don't care. I am out. Go fuck whoever you want."

He grabbed my arm hard with one hand, and with the other, he took a strong hold of my chin. It hurt.

"Why do you insist on making things complicated?" he said.

I stared at him, furious with hurt and rage, ready to fight him.

"I will tell you why! I am tired of your twisted games. You don't care about anyone else but yourself, you just use people. I have made many mistakes in my life. But you, you have been the worst. You think that because you are older and richer than me, you are better than me? Well, you are not! Good people don't cheat!"

I was telling Victor exactly what I should have told so many others in my life before him. "You are like a goddamn vampire bleeding people dry around you! Fuck you, fuck the Imperial. I'm out!" I shouted and struggled to get out of his grip.

He refused to let me go and held me even tighter in his grip. It felt like he was crushing my bones.

He was trying to talk calmly to me, but I could hear the anger in his voice. "I see the pattern now. You walk away as things get uncomfortable for you. You've lived in four or five countries in three years? You just get up and move to another country. Face the world! Stay and we will talk."

I had been held down by a guy before against my will; I knew exactly what to do next, when he wouldn't let me go. So, I breathed out and pretended to relax. Slowly, he let go of my hands. And I ran out.

• • • •

I WOKE UP BRUISED ON the inside and outside. I felt like I was made of glass, and every part of me had been shattered. I was going to hand in my notice today and move on. I was over this. I just wanted to move on to somewhere else. I intended to skip our morning meeting, but Matt saw me trying to get into the office without being noticed and called me out.

"We are all waiting for you, Leonora. Come on."

Reluctantly, I went into the staff room. They were all there. Hell, even Victor and Phillip. Phillip greeted me with a smile. I ignored Victor, but I could feel his burning stare. I sat down next to Maria, who made room for me.

"Phillip has his first official day as president today. He will get to know the different departments, by following each of you around. I would appreciate it if you showed him everything you think he should know about the guests and your workday. Thank you," Victor said without sounding appreciative at all.

The meeting seemed to take forever. I just wanted to get out and talk to Matt. The rage was still strong inside me.

Finally, the meeting came to an end, and I asked Matt for a quick meeting, just the two of us, before he left.

Victor quickly got up.

"Leonora, can I please have a word. I have an issue I need to talk to you about first."

I couldn't really decline the CEO in front of the others, so unwillingly, I walked to the corner of the room with Victor.

"Are you okay?" he lowered his voice so no one could hear us.

"Yes," I beamed, "why shouldn't I be?"

For once, I felt like I had the upper hand. "It had to end at some point, right, and I can feel that I am done now," I said defiantly.

His eyes were fixed on me. "We need to talk. Come by my office."

Nope, no chance, I thought to myself.

I turned my attention to Matt. "Can we talk now?"

He nodded, and we went back into our office.

"I know you, so before you speak, let me talk. Hasty decisions never leave to anything good."

I glared at him. "I am resigning. You know, you mean everything to me. But I want to leave. I know you are disappointed in me."

Matt smiled comfortingly at me. He was probably the same age as Victor, but much more like a father figure to me.

He sighed a few times. "Phillip is beginning to take over now as President, and I know they have great plans for you. Can we talk about this in a month?"

· · · ·

I STAYED IN THE OFFICE that day. Didn't even leave to go to the toilet or have lunch or dinner. Eventually, everyone had gone home, and it was dark and quiet on the floor. I went down to my secret hiding place and sought comfort in the dark while looking out of the window. The skyline was beautiful. The night sky was as dark as it could be here. I felt so overwhelmingly alone as I looked at the world's biggest city. Looking out on New York felt like being in a crowded room and yet feel completely lonely. Loneliness had been a companion of mine for so long that it made me feel comfortable, but tonight, it was just too much for me. Maybe this lifestyle wasn't for me after all. I let go of all the built-up frustrations and sobbed soundlessly for a while.

Suddenly, I could hear Victor on the phone. He walked agitatedly around in the corridor outside his office. He sounded angry and was very loud.

"The lawyers are working on it already. I don't care how they will solve it, I don't even care if it is through a hostile tender offer. The lawyers will decide. It will be done at the latest by the end of the year."

Then a long pause. "I know. I'm sorry, I am. They will be just fine. Stay away from the meeting if you want, but it will happen. I am chairman, CEO, and Head of the group. There is no point in trying to discuss it."

He hung up and hit the wall with his fist before he went into the elevator. I sat in the darkness for a while, before I went down to my room to sleep.

Chapter 5.

While Victor was away in Dubai, Phillip began to take on his role as president. He was a smart guy, and although he clearly wanted to take on the same leadership role as his older brother, he was still young and didn't have the same authority. But he was a sweet guy, and we all liked him.

Victor had been away for a week, when Phillip came into the lounge, greeting us with a seemingly heavy cardboard box. He put it on the bar.

"Newest edition of 'The New York Socialite', with our very own Victor on the frontpage. Please place them around the sitting area and in the library before we open today. Housekeeping is placing them in the rooms as well."

I didn't want to look in the magazine. Everybody else was busy going through the magazines. Out of the corner of my mind, I could see the cover was a teaser for an 8-page interview with Victor and Elizabeth on their upcoming wedding. I walked away. I could care less about their stupid wedding. Honestly, who actually cared. I didn't!

Phillip saw me walking away and came over to me.

"Victor is very impressed with you. He is usually not impressed by anyone, so it speaks volumes. Has he mentioned to you that he thinks you should be my executive assistant?"

I shook my head quietly. That proposition was most likely off the table now.

"Well, I would love to discuss some ideas with you and get them down on paper, so we can get things moving, so I will send you a meeting invite." I nodded.

· · · ·

THE DAYS PASSED QUIETLY without any big events. I would lie if I didn't admit that my heart was hurting. The burning anger had left me, and now only the cold ashes were left that had burned holes in my heart. I missed hearing his whisper in my ear, seeing the teasing smile on his lips, feeling his arms around me, his kisses, the way he would touch me, feeling him inside me, and our late-night conversations. I missed feeling protected and cared for. Even if it had all been a lie. I felt betrayed and worthless, despite I had known the rules of the game before we even began.

• • • •

TODAY WAS THE DAY VICTOR would be back from Dubai. I didn't even know if he would come back to act as CEO for the hotel chain or if he would leave it all to Phillip now. I just knew, for my own sanity, that I should stay far away. It was time to take control. And the only way, I knew how to, was to find someone new.

Maria and I walked arm in arm to the weekly staff meeting. Neither Phillip nor Victor was here. I let out a loud sigh of relief.

"This week we have a very important guest coming," Matt began, "old Mrs. Wetherill, widow of the late industry magnate Joseph Wetherill. She is also godmother to Phillip and Arthur Oppenheim, so you can understand that we have to take extra good care of her. She usually travels with a companion assistant, but due to an unexpected situation, she is coming alone. Leonora," everyone turned towards me, "you will be her companion. It's not about keeping her company 24-7, as she is here to visit both the Oppenheims and close relatives, but she has specifically requested for someone to take her out each day around New York."

Damian and Simon laughed out loud. Maria suggested I should entertain her with stories about the Civil War, and Leon recommended a poodle dog show. I looked at Matt for help. "Go talk to Phillip about ideas. He knows her. You can prepare today and tomorrow morning before she arrives and then present the ideas to her."

I wasn't overly keen on looking for Phillp in case I should run into Victor, so I stayed put and decided to do the research on my own without help.

Mrs. Wetherill was a fantastic lady. Phillip and Matt introduced me after her arrival and left us alone to plan the week. She was in her 70s, but she was bubbly, fun, and young at heart. Nothing you would have expected of a 70-year-old rich widow. I took an instant liking to her. I showed her my list of things, we could do, but she rejected all the ideas right away.

"I have seen it all. I am tired of being dragged to cultural places, just because I am old. You are a young, outgoing, beautiful woman. Take me where you would go, if you were planning a day out for yourself," she said.

"Well, I am not sure you would like the things, I would. I love escape rooms, and I have always wanted to try a rage room, and I could really need one today, so that is probably where I would go."

"I love it," she exclaimed. "Take me to a rage room and an escape room. It sounds like fun."

We laughed. This week might actually be fun and be all I needed to heal a broken heart.

Mrs. Wetherill was like a new best friend. We had a special chemistry, and by the end of the day after smashing things and yelling, and solving puzzles to avoid being killed by zombies, she was just Betty to me. This week would be fantastic! I went to bed with a smile on my face, and for once in these past two weeks, I wasn't angry, sad, or hurt when I fell asleep.

• • • •

I HAD PROMISED BETTY I would pick her up already in the morning, as she was eager for a new fun day together. She had breakfast in her room when I came to pick her up.

"So, you better bring extra underwear for today," I said jestingly. "I have arranged for a VR horror game. I am not even sure that I want to, but we have to try it."

I explained to her how we would wear a VR headset, and everything around us would change into a horrific world with zombies and monsters that we had to defeat. She thought it sounded amazing, so I ordered an Uber for us, and we went.

Side by side, with our headsets, we were transported into another realm. It was absolutely horrifying, and never in my life had I been so scared. We gasped, laughed, and screamed throughout the game, and when we finally took the headgear off, it felt like we had actually escaped death in real life. We went straight to the café next door, leaned back in the soft armchairs, ordered drinks, and giggled uncontrollably, feeling so elevated for having survived such a terrible experience.

"Thank you for taking me to these places," Betty said between some giggles. "It was what I needed. By the look of it, you did too. Would you like to talk about it?"

Betty was a fun best friend and a caring auntie in one, and for the first time in my life, I opened up completely to someone. I forgot all about professional protocol between staff and guests, and thankfully, she did too. I didn't mention Victor's name, but I told her about heartache and betrayal, about a dysfunctional upbringing, and about having tried to create a good life for myself, but failed again and again in desperate attempts to find happiness. She told me about her late husband and how lonely she had been for the past two years after his death.

We stayed in the small café ordering drinks and talking. Sometimes you meet someone and wish you were somehow related, so you would always be connected. That was how I felt about Betty. She didn't have any children on her own, she told me, so Phillip and Arthur had a special place in her heart. She told me how Phillip and Arthur walked in the shadow of a big brother who always did everything beyond expectations. I felt bad for Phillip. I could relate to his struggles, even if he had grown up in a privileged, rich home. Eventually, it was time to say goodbye for the day, as Betty had other engagements, so we went back to the Imperial and hugged goodbye.

I went down to my small, cozy room to read a book and listen to music. I couldn't concentrate on my book, though. The urge inside me to move on and find a new place to live was so strong. I wanted to leave so badly and get out of here, but Victor's words infuriated me, and I would prove him wrong and show him that he was so meaningless to me that I wouldn't leave at all.

· · · ·

I DIDN'T HAVE ANY PLANS with Betty the following day. Her schedule was busy, so instead Matt asked me to go through some old guest files. It was a tedious task, so I kept going down to Leon and Maria to chat. Maria was just telling me about a date she had been on last night, when someone called out my name. I turned around, and my blood froze to ice.

"Leonora, darling, come here," Betty called again. She was seated with Phillip, Arthur, presumably Arthur's girlfriend, the impeccable and stone-cold Elizabeth, and a woman with black hair that I guessed might just be Mrs. Oppenheim. And of course, Victor. Victor was back from Dubai, looking beautifully sun-kissed. I didn't think he could look any better. They had just finished lunch and were now having drinks and afternoon tea. A strange combination that rich people seemed to enjoy. Everyone was staring at me. Except for one person, of course. But I didn't care. Ghosting someone was my specialty, so he was up against the best.

"I was just telling them about all the fun we have had. I haven't laughed so much the past two years as I have these past two days with you. I can't wait to hear what we are doing tomorrow. Oh, by the way, Phillip has invited me on a helicopter sunset tour tomorrow evening! You must join us!"

I looked over at Phillip apologetic about crashing their date.

"You are more than welcome," he smiled at me.

Victor got up and left.

• • • •

BETTY AND I WENT INDOOR skydiving the next afternoon. I wish I would still be as adventurous when I was her age. Phillip picked us up from the skydive center and took us to a restaurant before the helicopter ride. Phillip and Betty were close to be a cure for a broken heart. Both were so witty, and I laughed so much that I snorted soda out of my nose. I flirted with Phillip, and enjoyed his obvious infatuation with me. It didn't heal my broken heart, but it felt like the broken pieces weren't as jagged. If I were to be executive assistant to the president, was it even fitting to be here, I thought to myself, but then again, I had reached a point where I didn't care anymore. If anyone had any complaints, I would be just fine leaving.

After some wrong turns, which left Phillip frustrated and Betty and me giggling, we finally made it to the building of the helicopter pad. We were warmly welcomed by the crew, who gave us a brief orientation. Once briefed, we made our way to the helicopter's landing pad. I had never flown in a helicopter before, and stepping inside the helicopter was a moment filled with nervousness for me. As the rotors whirred to life and the helicopter began to vibrate, I instinctively reached for something to hold on to. Realizing I had grabbed Phillip's thigh, I looked up and into his eyes to apologize, but the eyes that met me smiled at me, and he squeezed my hand comfortingly. Usually, I would have pulled my hand back, but his comforting hand was exactly what I needed, and so our hands stayed like that during the flight. As the sun began its descent, a warm golden glow fell upon the city. It was breathtaking and enchanting. Landmarks like the Statue of Liberty, Central Park, and Times Square were illuminated by the warm twilight, and watching the sun set on the city that never sleeps made New York seem even more fascinating. I could have stayed suspended over the city forever.

Once the helicopter tour was over, Betty and I said goodbye to Phillip to take an Uber back to the hotel. But as I was about to get into the car, Phillip called me.

"I have enjoyed your company today. I wondered if I could take you out on a date?" he asked.

"That's nice of you," I smiled politely. "Can I think about it and get back to you tomorrow?"

• • • •

I THOUGHT ABOUT IT the whole night. I tossed and turned. I liked being around Phillip, who was fun and outgoing. I was lonely, and I badly needed someone to hold me and heal me. Phillip could be the one, if I gave him a fair chance. Was it odd to date him when I had a history with his brother? Yes! But he would never have to know.

I met Phillip out in the corridor on my way to the staff meeting. We stopped and talked a bit about the day before.

"It would be nice to go on a date," I said and smiled at him.

He smiled back and told me he would pick me up at 6 p.m. if I could get an hour off earlier. I felt excited about going on a real date. I hurried in to ask Matt, before the staff meeting began. He would let me know at the meeting when he had time to look at everyone's schedules and the guest list, he promised.

The staff meeting was in the lounge today, as Matt wanted to go through trends in guest issues on this floor. Victor sat in an armchair in the corner with his laptop. I pretended not to see him. To me, he was invisible.

"Leonora, I have checked and it's fine, you can leave earlier tonight," Matt said at the start of the meeting.

"She has a date," Damian said teasingly. "And I also know with whom. But don't worry, baby, your secret is safe with me."

I looked at him, both surprised and anxious that he would spill my secret.

"I heard you talk before," he said, "you are going for the big guns, eh?"

I darted evil eyes at him, warning him to stay quiet. Everyone was watching the silent combat between us.

"Well, I don't care who finally won your heart, but I know one thing; Hearts are breaking all over the hotel tonight," Matt exclaimed.

I rolled my eyes with a smile. I could feel Victor's burning eyes on me.

Once the staff meeting was over, Matt asked me to write a summary for the staff to avoid future issues like the ones, he had gone through with us at the meeting, as well as plan some time in my schedule to coach the new staff. The task was quickly completed, and I went down to the reception to wait for Betty to take her out today. I had decided I would take her to City Island.

We began the day with a walk along the picturesque waterfront promenade. The calming sound of waves and the gentle sea breeze had a calming effect on me. I could live here forever. We wandered through the island's boutiques, art galleries, and antique shops before we visited the nautical museum. After lunch, I tried to convince Betty we should rent paddleboards, but she declined, and instead we enjoyed the water on a beautiful boat ride. It was hard to say goodbye to City Island, but we had to head back so I could get ready for my date.

. . . .

PHILLIP PICKED ME UP at the reception. "I'm taking you to the movies," he said excitedly. "So, we will just walk, if that is okay with you?" I nodded. I hadn't been to the movies in years, so I was equally excited. He bought me popcorn and soda and showed me to our seat, and it felt like a real teenage date. It was the kind of date I hadn't been on for years, and I enjoyed every second of it.

After the movie, he invited me to a nearby bar for a drink. Sensing the closeness of our first kiss, I turned to two glasses of rosé to calm my nerves. Phillip had a talent for easing the atmosphere by making jokes and making me giggle, but eventually, an awkward silence fell upon us. I recognized that silence from so many times before. I looked at him and smiled reassuringly. He took my hand and leaned in to kiss me. It wasn't a stolen, possessive, passionate kiss. It wasn't fireworks in the sky, but it was a soft and nice kiss. A kiss, I hoped wouldn't end soon. I moved toward him and pressed myself against him. I needed him. To kiss the pain away. We stayed at the bar for an hour more, just kissing. His soft lips caressed me like a gentle, soothing touch. Walking back to the hotel, we held hands. It really felt like a perfect teenage date from a movie.

I thought about inviting him back to my room; I really needed him to hold me tonight. But I knew it was highly inappropriate for someone in my position to drag someone back to my room, and even more so for the President to spend the night in a staff room. So, we kissed goodbye outside the hotel on the street.

• • • •

I WOKE UP FEELING EXCITED. I hoped to see Phillip today. As usual, I went to the gym to do my early morning training. Music was already on, when I got in, and I instinctively stepped back to go out again, but I couldn't see anyone, so I continued inside. Just as I closed the door behind me, I saw Victor on the pulldown machine. He was sweating, and his body glistened. I stared, paralyzed, at him. I felt like a fly trapped in a web. I knew I should get away quickly, but I couldn't move. Before my legs could finally move again, it was already too late, and he had seen me.

He got up, took his towel, dried his face and chest, and walked towards me. I wanted to look away, but I couldn't.

"I hear you are dating," he said with a bitter tone.

I didn't answer. There was nothing to say. He looked angry.

"With my brother, Leonora! With my fucking brother! Is it some kind of sick and twisted revenge? I knew you had issues, but this is beyond ridiculous. And what's your plan with him then? Fuck him and disappear? 'Leonora's Magic Disappearance Show begins very soon, ladies and gentlemen!'"

Victor was angry, but he had not seen how angry I could become, when I felt cornered. If he knew, he would not have started this. I unleashed all my built up hurt and anger and screamed every name I could think of at him. Eventually, I ran out of words, and switched to Danish to scream even more.

"Have you finished?" he hissed and grabbed my wrist. It hurt. "You are making a scene, and guests can hear you. Get yourself together."

"Jealousy doesn't become you, Victor," I said spitefully. I knew I was crossing a boundary by provoking the man who could fire me in one second.

"This is a joke! Are you a gold digger or just a slut?" he said with his eyes burning with anger. I tried to pull my hand back, but he held it harder. I hit him again and again on his chest with my fist, and he let my other hand go. He didn't try to stop me, but just took it. Slowly, the rage was over, and I felt so drained.

"Please, just let me try to be happy. You owe me that," I sobbed.

He pulled me in, and his intoxicating scent enwrapped me.

"Can we please talk?" he began.

I looked up at him and wiped my tears. In that moment, our eyes locked, and instinctively, our lips slowly met. Electricity bolted through my body. I did not want this, yet my whole body yearned for his touches. It was aching for him. I could feel my blood rushing and a tingling all over my body.

His phone rang. Of course, it did. It always did. Even this early in the morning. It was probably Maya or a fourth or fifth this time. Had all his business calls actually been business calls, or had they been a Maya? Now I remembered exactly why I hated him and ran out. He didn't try to stop me this time.

I slammed the door to my room as I came back. More determined than ever to forget his existence. I cried in the shower, but once I had finished washing my hair, I was ready to face the world. A world without Victor.

• • • •

A CERTAIN SOMEBODY, whose name I would not speak, had ruined my morning. My body was still shaking from my rage. Betty had plans for today, so I went to the office to write reports and drown my misery in tea. My phone rang. It was Leon asking me to come down to the bar, as Betty was looking for me.

"I'm taking my godsons out for lunch today. Please join us."

I was more than happy to leave my reports at the desk, so Betty and I went down to the reception to wait for an Uber.

"We are having lunch at the Parkview Palace," she laughed. "I stay in one hotel and eat in another."

Arthur was already seated with his girlfriend in the beautiful restaurant. She seemed like a sweet girl. Her appearance and manners revealed she was of a wealthy family, but unlike a certain impeccable woman, Charlotte was much more pleasing and friendly. Phillip was happy to see me, and I noticed he and Betty exchanged a wink. Arthur and Phillip were joking and teasing each other through lunch. Imagine growing up in a happy home and never having to worry about money. Our lives were so different.

"So, how is Victor doing? Your mother called me last night and was worried," Betty interrupted my thoughts.

Was she asking me? Arthur stopped teasing his girlfriend and answered Betty.

"All I know is that he is in a bad mood lately. There is a lot going on. Did mama tell you?"

"Yes, she mentioned it," Betty replied.

I didn't know what they were talking about.

"I hope he doesn't sabotage the upcoming wedding. Loreen is really hoping for grandchildren soon," Betty smiled.

I felt sick.

"Yeah, let's see," Phillip said looking thoughtful. "Dad is furious, but there is really nothing he can do, so we will all back up Victor's decision and hope for the best. Victor never makes a wrong decision, so I trust him on his one as well."

I didn't care about it, so I excused myself and got up to go to the toilet. When I came back, they had thankfully moved on to more interesting and fun topics. It was a nice lunch, and I felt so happy, I reached out to hold Phillip's hand. He looked at me with a smile.

Phillp took us back to the hotel to say goodbye to Betty. Betty's stay at the Imperial was over, and I would miss her dearly. She had been fun, and she had been like a bandage on a bleeding wound. Not enough to heal or stop the bleeding, but enough to cover it, so it was easier to forget about it.

Chapter 6.

Phillip and I had been on four dates. He was a sweet guy who made me laugh, and I liked how he made me feel special, when he took me out on dates. We hadn't slept together. I wasn't in a rush, I just enjoyed the laughs and the soft kisses, and Phillip seemed like a true gentleman who didn't push things. I was 21 years old. Of course, I knew we couldn't continue to just hold hands and kiss, and I didn't want to either; the fire that Victor had lit inside me was burning and needed to be put out. I only hesitated because everything was just a turmoil inside me, and I needed things to be simple right now.

The hotel was busy today. We had lawyers coming in and out of the board room, and the library was closed off for internal meetings as well. Men in suits whispered discreetly while walking back and forth between the rooms. I saw both Victor, Mr. Oppenheim, Arthur, and Phillip in the meetings. In between meetings, Phillip found me.

"We are going to have meetings all day long and tomorrow as well, but can we meet out on the terrace perhaps tonight?"

"Of course," I replied with a smile.

The meetings went on into the evenings, and I was tired, but I had promised to wait for Phillip out on the terrace, so I cuddled under a blanket with the lit-up night sky above me.

"There you are! I am so tired, but I am glad you waited for me," he said as he appeared in the door. I opened my blanket and invited him in with me. Phillip kissed me softly on the lips. He had the softest kisses that made me smile each time. I needed him. I wanted him to take me as passionately as I had been taken over and over just a few weeks ago. I kissed him passionately, moved my hands down to his pants, and began to open his belt.

"Here? Are you sure?" he whispered.

I looked at him teasingly and smiled.

"There is no one else here, and we can just hide under the blanket." I continued to unbutton his pants. I needed him now.

"Sorry, I should have been prepared. I don't have a condom with me. I can try to get one."

He got up. He came back with a condom. We kissed again, and I pulled him down to me, teasing and kissing him under the blanket.

"Would you like me to put it on now?" he whispered.

I nodded.

I am not quite sure what happened next. Before we even had begun, I heard someone or something. Phillip got up quickly and said something, but I couldn't see why. I pulled the blanket around me, confused.

"Was it a nice fuck?" Victor moved past Phillip and stared at me.

Philip looked at Victor, back at me, then back at Victor. The two brothers exchanged glances. Phillip looked back at me in disbelief.

"I should have known. Victor was here before me. You know that he has a fiancée and still sleeps around with half of the city? I don't understand why you all fall for it. I thought you were better than that, Leonora."

Touché. That hurt. How could I explain to Phillip that Victor was like a deadly virus inside my body, that I couldn't find a cure, and now I was left dying on the inside. That I so desperately wanted to like someone else but him, but I couldn't. I couldn't explain all this, but I would not allow Victor to try to destroy my chance of happiness. He had no right to do so.

I looked at Victor defiantly. "We didn't fuck. We made love." And with a knife, I twisted the final words into his heart. "With a condom."

We were even now, yet I felt defeated. Phillip stood there, baffled. I rearranged my shirt and skirt and put my shoes back on.

"Stand back and watch, Phillip. What you are about to witness is 'Leonora's Great Disappearance Show' that begins now!" Victor sneered at me.

Phillip looked like he had been hit by an invisible bus and didn't say anything, still just looking at us, but suddenly something seemed to dawn on him. He shook his head in disbelief.

"That's why? She is the reason? I just realized it now, Victor! This is what it's all about! You are an asshole! You had so many chances to tell me!" he shouted.

I didn't care about their argument; my war was with Victor. Who the fuck was he to talk to me like that. I sent an angry glare at Victor and walked out. I didn't care if I had detonated an atomic bomb between two brothers.

I was so caught up in anger. I couldn't go back to my room. I just couldn't. I didn't want to be on my own. I thought about waking Maria, but I couldn't tell her what had happened with Phillip or Victor. I was all alone, and I only had myself to blame. I went to my secret hideout on the 17th floor and laid down on a soft sofa with plush cushions. It never ended well for me, and now I've messed this up as well. I wanted to go back to England. I was sure I could get my old job back. But maybe it was time to leave the hotel world. I fell asleep on the sofa with thousands of thoughts going through my mind.

. . . .

I HAD A TERRIBLE HEADACHE when I woke up. I went down to my room to get ready. I skipped breakfast because I wasn't in the mood to talk to anyone. I went straight to the office to hide from the world.

"Oh, you look terrible today, Leonora. Are you ill?" Matt asked with concern.

"No, just a headache, I'm fine."

"Listen, we have one week left before the holidays. You get a whole week off where you can relax and have fun, so put on your smile and charm the guests. Are you going home?"

"I can't leave the country, you know. Immigration will never let me in again. So, I thought I would go somewhere nice and warm, like Florida perhaps."

"I forgot about that. You can't spend Christmas on your own, Leonora."

"It's fine. It's not the first Christmas, I have spent alone, I don't mind it."

Matt smiled comfortingly at me. "Sometimes your independence makes things harder for you."

I sighed.

I had to get one thing done today to make me feel just a little bit better. I got up, walked down the corridor, and knocked on the door. I was nervous.

"Come in," Phillip said and opened the door for me.

He didn't look too good either.

He gestured to the sofa. "We can sit here."

A long pause between us. I inhaled to speak.

"No, listen. I will speak first. I didn't mean to be mean to you last night. I'm sorry for what I said. I'm not blind to Victor's looks and charm and how women throw themselves at him. I get it. I like you and thought this could have led to something. You should have played with open cards from the beginning.

I can't win when it comes to him, and I don't even want to try, and it upsets me that I didn't even know I was up against him," he said.

I honestly didn't care anymore. I nodded and held back my tears.

"Have you talked to Victor this morning?" he asked.

I shook my head. I had nothing more to say to Victor.

"I thought he would have talked to you. I told him to last night. Anyway, the story will be out today, so I might as well tell you. We did it. Or Victor did. His father-in-law, Mr. Phillips, is out of the Oppenheim Group now. He was forced out. Victor convinced the majority of the shareholders to force the sale of Mr. Phillips' shares. And the shares we had in his company have been sold. All ties have been cut. It will create turmoil on the stock market today, and we will probably have journalists trying to come in. We will have a staff meeting later."

I didn't care about the stock market. Or who owned what. All I cared about was that I had lost once again. Even if Phillip was probably not the one for me, I still enjoyed our dates and how he made me laugh all the time. And I really needed that right now. But as Matt had said, I just had to survive one week, and then I was off for a week.

It was a chaotic day. We did have journalists trying to sneak in, hoping they could find Victor, or Phillip or anyone else with insider knowledge. We were told to discard the newspapers that had stories about the situation, so we didn't have the guests making a fuss out of it. It seemed crazy to me, but I didn't care about pieces of paper or who owned how many. Apparently, the one behind it all had gone to Dubai for the next couple of weeks to finish the projects, the company had there. I still didn't care.

. . . .

FINALLY, IT WAS THE last day before the hotel closed for the holidays. Everybody was excited to go home. I packed all of my things, not sure if I would return. I hugged Maria and promised I would send her a letter, if I didn't return.

"You are the only person left on this planet without a mobile," she joked.

I did have a mobile. I had just never gotten around to getting an American SIM card, and one day took the other, and I realized I had no one to call outside of work, so what difference did it make.

* * * *

I WENT TO FLORIDA AS planned. I stayed until the beginning of January, as I wasn't ready to face the chaos in New York just yet. My New Year's resolution was to grow roots somewhere and find a nice, decent guy. I would see if I could somehow become a legal immigrant and study hotel management in New York. That way I could keep Matt, Maria, and Damian in my life. It was getting too hard to start over all the time and leave good friends behind, knowing you would never see them again, because you live in different countries. Maria was the first one I ran to see, when I came back. We hugged for so long.

"Damian and I were sure you wouldn't come back. We already had a search and retrieve plan ready."

We laughed.

Matt was happy to see me too, and I felt really good about my decision to stay here and try to settle down. "I am glad you are back! Phillip has asked if you could take on the role of his executive assistant when you came back. Are you still interested?"

So, Phillip wasn't mad at me. I felt a bit hurt that he apparently was so fine with it all, but also relieved that we were okay.

"Yes, that would be great, thank you," I beamed.

"Well, let's go find Phillip and your new office. I will miss sharing an office with you. But I feel like a proud dad right now; I took you in as a lost waitress, and look at you now."

I giggled. This would be my perfect year. The year that everything would go just as planned.

* * * *

PHILLIP AND I WERE a great team. Phillip was still young and insecure in his role as president, but he was hardworking and determined to do his best. Victor had left him a hotel business in healthy condition with a solid economy and growth, and our priority was expanding and continuing the growth. I could tell Phillip had the support of his father and Victor; I heard him on the phone with them almost every day. I never asked him about Victor, and by the sound of it, Victor never asked about me either. The rumor mill, however, was busy

as always, so I heard that the engagement had been broken off. I hoped that he was lonely, but he probably had three naked girls in his bed.

Chapter 7.

As winter's grip tightened at the beginning of February and left New York City covered in snow, it brought back memories from my childhood playing in the snow with my brother and my friends. How I once built an igloo for my rabbit, that time my best friend and I walked over the frozen lake home just to see what the fuzz was about, when I got my first pair of skis, and all the snowmen my brother and I built in our garden. I welcomed the invigorating cold on my cheeks. I even persuaded Leon, Maria, Simon, and Damian to a snow fight out on the terrace late at night.

With February came Valentine's Day. To avoid feeling alone on the most romantic day of the year, I volunteered to work the evening shift in the lounge, so those with a date could have the evening off. I was happy that I did. The atmosphere was magical on February 14. A pianist and harpist provided a melodious, romantic backdrop throughout the day and evening. The floor was adorned with delicate pink rose petals, and beautiful red roses stood on every table. The lovely scent of roses was amazing and created an extraordinary atmosphere. We had a professional photographer to capture the couple's special moments, and as couples left, they received a small bouquet of red roses from us. It was amazingly romantic, and I was so thrilled to be a part of it. Until that moment. That moment when Victor came in with his date. I hadn't seen him since that night. And now he came waltzing in with a new girl, like the dog he was. I quickly looked at the list, and thankfully, he was not seated in my area. I breathed a sigh of relief. Fine, that meant I could ignore him and pretend he was invisible. And I did a remarkably good job throughout the night, if I had to say so myself.

"Either you are a terrible waitress or you are trying to pretend I am not here."

I didn't want to turn around and face the voice. I was clearing a table in a quiet corner of the lounge, where no one could save me from a conversation, I did not want to take part in. "Either way, it is not a good look when I'm the CEO."

I turned around.

I avoided looking him in the eyes and shrugged my shoulders. "Well, I am sorry for my lack of waiting skills. I will be more attentive."

He chuffed. "Can we talk?"

I nodded. I didn't care anymore. Discreetly, we walked out of the lounge and up to my office on the floor above. We stood in silence for a while.

"I always made love to you ," he said quietly.

I wasn't prepared for this conversation.

"You made me feel so cheap, and stupid, and naïve and worthless," I said getting myself worked up again.

He cleared his throat. "I would really like to explain and give you my side of the story, but now is not the right time. Can we talk tomorrow?"

"It's fine. We don't need to talk. It's fine. All is good. You have a Valentine's date. Go back to her."

"Leonora, you drive me crazy! Of course, tomorrow you will probably be running for the hills, so fine, let's talk now. I was suggesting to do it tomorrow out of respect for the fact that you are actually on a shift on the busiest day of the year, and probably have tables waiting for you right now," he looked at me quite annoyed.

He took my phone, dialed the number to the lounge and said, "Leonora is on a break. Get someone to take over her tables now, thank you."

He hung up.

"Fine, let's talk now. Who starts?" he asked.

"I think I have said all I needed to say."

I looked at him and sat down on the sofa with my arms crossed.

"Okay, so I made you feel cheap and stupid and worthless, right?"

I didn't move.

"For that I am sorry. I am."

He sat down next to me. "I never made a promise to be faithful to you. You knew I had a fiancée, and I told you repeatedly not to get emotionally involved, so it seems a bit unreasonable to start World War III because of a phone call from a woman."

Just like that, he made me feel stupid and worthless again. I looked away.

"I never used a condom with you, because..." he paused, "because you were different. This between us was different. Had I known how much it meant to you, I would have. Of course, I would have. But it didn't feel right with you.

I always use a condom. But our connection was different, and I wanted to be closer to you. Did I sleep with others while I slept with you? Yes. Not because you were worthless, or because you were just another number. I have cheated on Elizabeth for years, I admit that. That was different. I slept with someone else maybe twice during the time, we were together. Honestly, you drove me crazy. You were always on my mind. I couldn't concentrate. I had to try to get my mind off of you. I didn't sleep with them, because I needed something else or was led astray. I did it because I liked you too much. You messed everything up, set my world on fire. I changed the whole setup of the company and shook its foundation just to be with you. And then you threw yourself a Phillip. My own brother. That is disturbing."

I still didn't know what to say. I would have liked an agenda for this meeting beforehand, so I could have come prepared. I felt dizzy. His perfume was musky and sensual. He was sitting close to me, and I could feel his warmth. Our knees touched, sending a subtle yet electrifying sensation coursing through me. I looked down at his hands and his muscular arms. I remembered how those hands had been all over my body, and how his arms had held me down during passionate encounters. A small, yet intimate smile spread on his lips.

"You are not paying attention. I know that look." He put his hand on my thigh and hesitated for a second, before he began to kiss my neck. I closed my eyes and leaned my head back. No! Fool on me for giving in so quickly.

"Who is your date?" I asked and broke free.

"She is not important to you. It's just a casual date," he said and tried to kiss my neck again. "And Elizabeth?"

He sighed and looked me in the eyes. "Listen...I have known her for years. Our fathers are good friends, and our businesses had intertwined. She is the perfect New York socialite, and she seemed like the perfect choice for me. I got involved with her, because it was the right thing for my family and our company. Then I met you. I didn't know someone like you existed. You are like a drug to me. You are funny, smart, and kind, and I love talking to you. You have been on my mind ever since I saw you the first time. And I can't get enough of you," he pulled me closer.

"But you never told me this—"

"I was engaged. We were preparing the wedding of the year. Her father had a large share in our company, and we had the same in his. I couldn't just get out.

I couldn't promise you anything. I didn't know if we could successfully take over his shares and sell ours. It takes a lot of work for lawyers. And when, we finally did it, you were fucking my brother. Or let me rephrase that, you made love to my brother."

He grasped the back of my neck hard and pulled my head back to bite me in my neck. It wasn't a purely loving gesture. It felt like punishment.

"You really fucked up on this one. I can't believe I would ever be that crazy for someone to let something like that go. And I haven't heard one apology yet!"

"Victor, you are hurting me," I whimpered. "I'm sorry. I needed someone so badly to comfort me, and he was there, and he was kind and sweet, and all that I needed right then. I hated you. I thought I would never talk to you again. But you interrupted us just before...you know we didn't have sex, right?"

He looked up at me with surprise. He didn't know. He let out a sigh of relief. He marked me by biting and sucking my neck passionately, while his hands gripped my thighs tight.

"I've always had great timing," he said with a grin as he tore my shirt open. Always so skillful.

He squeezed my breasts hard, sucked and bit my nipples. I breathed heavily. I let my fingers run down his thighs, and he quickly unbuttoned his shirt and took it off. I gripped him by his belt and pulled him down towards me. I opened his pants and leaned back on the sofa, ready for him.

He pulled a condom out of his pocket. "Would you like me to use it?"

I shook my head with a smile. I wanted to feel him come inside me.

"Such a big fuss for something you didn't even want," he said and kissed me passionately.

I scratched his back with my nails, as he slowly entered me. Then, I wrapped my arms and legs around him. He couldn't move properly in my hold, so we stayed like that, kissing intertwined with him inside me. It felt so unbelievably intense, and I could feel small contractions inside me holding him tight.

"I want to take you from behind. Can I?" he whispered in my ear.

I nodded. He sat up, lifted my legs up to his shoulder, and used a hand cream, I had next to the sofa, to lubricate, before he gradually and slowly pushed himself in between my butt cheeks. I tried to relax and breathe slowly, but the intensity of it was so strong. Calmly, he moved in and out of me. I let out a deep moan, grasping his hands. Our fingers interlocked while we were connected in a mutual gaze. He let one hand go and gently let his fingers play with me. He knew exactly where to find the right spot, sending shivers through my body. Our eyes were locked.

"You have to come now. I can't hold it," he gasped.

He tried to control himself and do it slowly, but his pounding got quicker and harder as he came closer to his climax. I gasped for air, feeling how he swelled inside me before I felt his warm explosion. I screamed out while every cell in my body seemed to ignite and send sparks throughout my body. He pulled out of me kissing me gently all over my body. I smiled in satisfaction.

"In the Badlands," I began to explain, "it was my first time—"

"I know. I'm sorry that you thought my heart was not in it, and I didn't make you feel safe. But I am glad, you are smiling this time," he said and winked at me."I will give you so many first times your head will spin."

We lay there for a while.

"By the way, happy Valentine's Day. Next year, I would prefer you do not ignore your CEO. Actually, I don't think the CEO's girlfriend should work at all on Valentine's Day. I'm sure there is somewhere on your bucket list, we could be instead."

I looked at him and blushed. Did he really just call me his girlfriend? And plan next year? Could this really be my happy ending?

"I'm taking you on a date in the morning. Phillip can do without you. I have somewhere I have wanted to take you."

I just felt so happy. Victor and I on a proper date. I was curious to see where he was taking me, and he could tell by my expression.

"I'm taking you to the Houdini Museum. I'm sure you will feel right at home at his museum," he laughed, "But don't get any ideas, though. I seriously hate how you try to run away all the time. We need to work on that."

I giggled, and he smiled at me. "Actually, we are taking the week off. I know your bucket list is long, so we better start now ticking places off."

We kissed. Incessantly. Passionately.

THE END.

• • • •

DID YOU ENJOY THE BOOK? I hope you did. Please be so kind to give it an honest review where you bought it. I would be forever grateful as it allows me to continue writing these stories ♥

Don't miss out!

Visit the website below and you can sign up to receive emails whenever Nora O. Eigil publishes a new book. There's no charge and no obligation.

https://books2read.com/r/B-A-LTEAB-QOJNC

BOOKS 2 READ

Connecting independent readers to independent writers.